DOUBLE TROUBLE

BY

DARCY FLYNN

ACKNOWLEDGMENTS

Many thanks to my wonderful critique partners, Cindy Brannam and Jeanne Hardt. From the brainstorming stage to the final critique, your thoughtful input always makes me think.

To my editor, Ally Robertson, as always your attention to detail, and your insightful suggestions, made my book even better. Your editorial intuition always amazes me. Thank you.

Tom and Roman, you both know what your support and encouragement mean to me. Thank you!

Dedication

Some of my dearest friends have been identical twins - for as far back as I can remember, to now. Six sets, to be exact. I've always loved being the *one* who could tell you apart, the best friend who shared your secrets and your pranks.

I thought it was time I dedicated a book to you. You know who you are!

CHAPTER ONE

"Oh, my gosh." Megan's eyes widened. "That's him. That's Carrington."

"He's here?" Clare Sullivan shifted in her seat for a better look.

So that was the man who'd called her billionaire sister a gold digger.

Since he was perusing the lunch menu, Clare did a bit of perusing herself. Even in thoughtful study of the menu, he eclipsed the other two men seated at his table. He wore a light gray suit, and his dark hair was neatly trimmed. He possessed an air of self-assurance she normally would have admired in anyone else.

Why was it always the attractive, impeccably dressed and amazingly fit men who believed an equally attractive, and flawlessly dressed woman could only be after their fortune? Or, in this case a younger brother's inheritance.

Seriously, did they all think a woman could only gain wealth by marrying some old geezer on his deathbed? Not that the man sitting mere feet away from her was old or a geezer. On the contrary, he was every bit the opposite.

Megan stared down at her plate and fiddled with her pizza crust. Her younger sister's pout reminded her that a man's looks were not everything, and rarely could he be trusted for what was underneath.

"Are you sure that's Chris's brother?"

Megan raised blue eyes to Clare. "I could only see his profile, but I'm certain that's him." She shivered. "After he called me a gold digger, he told Chris not to bring any more like *me* to their island."

If this was an example of the "Carrington" charm, her sister was well rid of them. Clare hadn't been keen on Megan going alone to some bachelor's island during spring break anyway, but there were other, less hurtful ways to un-invite someone. *But, seriously? Gold Digger?* Her half-sister could buy ten islands with her inheritance.

Greek salad and half-eaten sausage pizza, now cold from neglect, permeated her senses. Clare pressed her lips firmly together and gazed across the table at Megan. Clare had hoped after Megan's semester in college, raising her would have become easier. But, her sister's delicate crease of an-noyance between her brow clearly said Clare's job was far from finished.

Having lost their parents ten years earlier when she was sixteen and Megan ten, Clare had fired the nanny. With the help of their beloved butler, she had raised her sister. From that point on, her life was consumed with studying, and with Megan. As co-heir to the Pendelikon fortune, she lacked for nothing, except a date on Friday nights.

Now, she was one of the most sought after home designers in South Florida, but sadly lacked experience when it came to men.

Stomach acid churned Clare's midsection. She so wished she'd had the nerve to give this Carrington a piece of her mind. But, Clare didn't lose control.

Ever.

She sucked in a calming breath and reached inside her purse for an antacid. For the moment, thinking daggers into his heart would have to suffice.

She chewed the chalky tablet and eyed her half-sister. It had been a decade since their parents' accident, and she'd championed Megan, taking on role of protector and mother ever since. They'd had such a nice morning shopping along Fifth Avenue South, finishing up the outing here at Osteria Tulia for one of Chef Betulia's famous pizzas. She hated it had to end on such a sour note.

Megan tossed her napkin on the table and stood. "Excuse me."

"Sure, honey."

Megan hurried off to the restroom. Poor kid, she was obviously upset. They should leave. After she motioned to her waiter to bring the bill, she glanced at the other two men seated with Carrington. They were also in suits.

Wait, she knew one of them.

Kenneth Barton from Caldwell Developers.

She quickly glanced at the bathroom entrance and still, no Megan. Taking a chance Megan would be a bit longer, she stood and crossed the short distance to the table where the gentlemen were seated.

"Ken?"

He glanced up and immediately smiled. "Clare. My goodness." He stood and held out his hand. "It's great to see you."

"It's good to see you, too." She shook his hand.

"How long's it been? Six, seven months?"

"Yes. About." She smiled.

"Will, Dave, this is Clare Sullivan," Ken said. "She's a designer with Lot's House Designs."

"*Former* designer," she corrected him. "I'm on my own now."

"That doesn't surprise me," he said.

She nodded toward Dave, then turned her attention to Will.

"This is such a coincidence," Ken said. "Will was just saying that he needed to find a decorator for his new penthouse."

Clare raised her brow and looked right into the gorgeous, self-assured face of Will Carrington. He eyed her with an appreciative gleam, stood, and extended his hand.

"Is that right?"

"It is." She placed her hand in his, surprised that such a warm, gentle pressure could belong to such a heartless creature.

Was it her imagination or did Will cling to her fingers a fraction longer than necessary? His direct gaze mesmerized and, for a moment, rendered her speechless. And those violet eyes… She swallowed and pulled her hand away. Will smiled, and Clare's knees buckled. *Dazzling.* No other word came to mind. If the younger Carrington's smile was anything like the older brother's, she could certainly see how her eighteen-year-old sister had lost her heart.

"Do you have a card?" Will said.

Clare slipped one from the pocket of her silk dress and handed it to him. His warm fingers brushed against hers, and tingles skipped up her arm. She snatched her hand away as if she'd touched fire. His fine lips quirked. Warmth flushed her cheeks. She took a controlling breath, despising herself for her schoolgirl reaction.

"Well." Her glance encompassed the group. "Don't let me disturb you any longer. I just wanted to say hi. Enjoy your lunch."

The three men stood as she turned away. Clare grabbed her purse, slipped cash into the plastic folder that housed the bill, then left. She met Megan at the entrance right as she came out of the restroom.

"I thought you might want to leave," Clare said.

"You thought correctly." Megan shot her a brief smile and skirted the waiting crowd to the entrance of the restaurant.

Megan sat quietly in the seat next to Clare on the drive back home, periodically swiping at a tear. "Why would he even say such a thing about me? He doesn't even know me."

Clare huffed out a sigh. "Do you want me to go back and sock him one?"

Megan giggled on a half sob. "No. Besides, that's something more like what *I'd* do."

"Don't I know it."

It was actually more like her than Megan realized. Upon the news of their parents' tragic death, she'd immediately outgrown her impulsive streak. Done. Over. She was never the same.

She turned into the parking garage and pulled her practical, blue Prius into one of four slots marked Pendelikon. Her little gas-saving car looked ridiculously out of place sandwiched between the family Bentley and Megan's vintage Corvette.

Clare switched off the engine right as Megan glanced in her direction. "Seriously, you've got to get a different car. This is borderline embarrassing."

"It's practical for my work."

"Until you need to cart a piece of furniture to someone's house."

"And when I do, I just fold the back seats forward, and there's plenty of room."

Megan placed her hand over Clare's. "Why not get an SUV. An Audi or a Lexus. They hold a ton of stuff."

Clare shrugged. "I like my little car."

Megan pursed her lips. "You like punishing yourself."

Clare glanced at Megan, whose wide, stricken eyes locked onto hers.

"Oh, Clare. I'm so sorry. That came out all wrong. I just meant...I just wish you'd quit blaming yourself. It's okay to use his money. It's now *your* money. He left it to you."

Clare gave Megan a half smile and pulled her hand away. "I've made my decision. Now, let's not talk about it."

"Okay. Fine." Megan pushed open the car door and got out.

Clare clicked the lock button on her key chain as she maneuvered her body sideways between her car and the Bentley. "Look, I know you're disappointed about Chris." She hoped the change in subject would refocus Megan on something other than their father. "We'll finish our shopping later and plan your revenge. How about it?"

"And salvage my spring break with new clothes? That sounds suspiciously like a bribe to me." Megan struck a pose. "You know me so well."

Clare was rewarded with Megan's cagy grin. Mention the word "shopping," and the world became a brighter place. Over the years, Clare had learned that word held magical powers over her younger sister. Subsequently, she'd used it often. As a result, Megan had turned into a bit of a spendthrift. Completely Clare's own fault, of course. But it always cheered her, and it wasn't like they couldn't afford it.

As they crossed the concrete floor to the penthouse elevator, Clare thought about her earlier encounter with Will Carrington. The appreciative gleam in his eyes had held her spellbound, his devilish smile adding a roguish twinkle to their depths. The sudden image of a pirate loomed in her line of vision.

Would she have confronted him if Ken and the other man hadn't been there? The old Clare certainly would have. The old Clare would've shaken her fist in his irritatingly fine-looking face. Told him exactly what she'd thought of him and his comments.

The elevator doors closed, and she let out a sigh.

"Go ahead and say it," Megan said.

"Say what?"

"That it was stupid to pretend I was poor. That it backfired just like you warned it would."

"Any girl who drives a vintage Corvette is *not* poor."

Megan shrugged.

"And I *never* said it was stupid," Clare added. "Certainly not the best idea you've ever had, but—"

Megan spun toward her. "For once in my life, I just wanted someone to like me... *love* me, for me. Not Daddy's millions."

"It's actually billions, honey."

"Whatever. You know what I mean."

The elevator opened to a wide foyer. A round antique walnut table graced the center of the room with an arrangement of fresh flowers.

Edward, their long time butler, crossed the marble floors to greet them. "How was lunch?"

"Lovely, thank you," Clare said. "And you really don't need to keep meeting us at the door," she lovingly chided, while Megan continued on to her bedroom.

"As you keep telling me." He tilted his head in deference to her.

"You practically raised us. A hug would definitely be in order," she teased.

He raised a shaggy brow. "What would your father think?"

"Technically, he was *not* my father." She smiled, hoping to lessen the blow to his sensibilities. Edward had been in America for years, but was still *very* British and quite proper.

"I was with Mr. Pendelikon for twelve years before he met and married your mother. He always considered you his daughter."

"I know he did. He's the only father I ever knew, and I loved him, but that doesn't mean you are to treat us like him. Don't you want your own life?"

"The Pendelikons *are* my life." With those final words, he excused himself.

"Oh, Edward?"

He stopped in his tracks and turned around.

"My new assistant, Brenda Simpson, was supposed to stop by this morning at ten. I hired her last week to help with my overflow. Sorry, I meant to tell you sooner. She was supposed to take a look at the Howards' file."

"Yes. Miss Brenda was most punctual and told me she scribbled some notes in the margins for you."

Clare entered her home office, where her latest client's file was spread out over her desk. She picked up Brenda's notebook. Talk about scribble. Angling her head to the side, Clare did her best to decipher Brenda's handwriting. She finally gave up and stood over the collection of paint chips and fabric swatches, playing with the Howards' color pallet.

They'd been a joy to work with, eager for her suggestions and open to her ideas. She wished all her clients were so agreeable. Several of them ignored her input to such an extent she wondered why they'd hired her in the first place.

Her cell phone rang, and she glanced at the caller ID. Speaking of which...

"Hi, Laney."

"Clare. The upholsterer just arrived, and he covered the chair in the wrong fabric. I specifically wanted the yellow and white stripe."

Clare groaned inwardly. "We changed it to the gold and white, remember? Especially since you insisted. You said the yellow was too bright next to the floral sofa. But, I think the—"

"We discussed that, yes. But then decided the *yellow* and white was better because it blended with the wall treatment."

"The walls in the living room are painted. The wall treatment you're referring to is for the Master bedroom."

"Oh, that's right. I forgot. But I still don't like the gold stripe on this chair."

As I tried to tell you.

"That's fine. Put Theo on the phone."

Clare wanted to cuss. A darn string of cuss words, but she held her tongue.

"Theo. I'm so sorry. Take the chair back to your shop, and I'll order the yellow stripe for her. We'll do it her way."

"Yes, ma'am."

Laney got back on the phone. "Are we all set?"

"Yes. Theo will take the chair back, and I'll order the other fabric this afternoon."

Clare pressed *end*, then punched in the number for the Dayna Embrey rep. She placed the order for the yellow and white stripe, then made her way to the kitchen for a cool drink. After mixing orange juice and Perrier over ice, she plopped herself down on the cream linen sofa in the family room.

She took a long drink, then rested her head against the goose down cushion. She was still furious with Laney, who'd cost Clare more than once with her indecisive screw-ups. But not this time. This time the mistake was clearly Laney's, and Clare wasn't about to pay for another one.

She still wanted to cuss, or at least kick something. She blew out a frustrated breath. When all of her friends were coming of age and taking on the culture around them, Clare hadn't followed the pack. She had a little sister to raise. After their parents had died, she'd taken on the re-sponsibility, determined to set the example her sister needed, and never looked back. Megan adored her, and she couldn't let her down, or her parents. She could not, *would* not, disappoint them.

The Pendelikon fortune was left equally in trust to the two of them. Clare still felt her share was undeserved and had refused to access it when she'd turned twenty-five. One, she was not James Pendelikon's daughter. And two, it was her fault he and her mother were dead.

* * *

Will Carrington tapped the edge of Clare Sullivan's business card against his desk. Even though lunch was hours ago, her sparkling eyes continued to accuse him. But accuse him of what? She'd certainly been angry, but talk about control. This woman had it in spades. But, she couldn't have been angry with him? He didn't even know her. Had only just met her. However, he found himself *wishing* he'd been the cause.

He raised the card to his lips. Truthfully, he'd like nothing better than to take her in his arms and kiss that pent-up regression right out of her. He shook his head and stood.

He yanked open the door to his office. "Carol." He crossed the carpet to his assistant's desk and handed her the business card. "Call Miss Sullivan and set up an appointment for her to come by. I'd like to talk to her about my house."

"Which one?"

"Miami."

"Ah, the infamous penthouse." She smiled. "So you decided to keep it after all?"

"And listen to my brothers carry on about my bohemian beach lifestyle?" He grinned. "No thank you."

As he approached his car, he punched in Chris's number. It rang twice before his youngest brother picked up.

"Wes tells me you've gotten yourself another gold-seeking girlfriend. What's all this about?"

"She's not a gold digger. She's adorable. And I think I love her."

"They're all adorable. And you thought you *loved* the redhead. What was her name? Minnie?"

Chris huffed out a breath, and Will could just imagine the expression on his brother's face. He'd seen it many times before. Clenched jaw, lips tightly pressed together, and the stubborn jut of his Carrington chin.

"Minnie was ages ago."

"Okay. Fine." Will sighed. "What's this new girl like?"

That's all the invitation it took for Chris to spill his heart out. Will listened patiently to a long litany of descriptive words like adorable smile, sparkling eyes, and hot body.

"The first time I saw her I knew this one was different. And I can tell she likes me for me and not for my money."

"And how would you know? Did you ask her?"

"Of course not. Look. She likes me. She's interested in *me*. She never once asked what my father did."

"That's why Google exists."

"Very funny."

"Does she know your father's dead?"

"Yes and so is hers, by the way. We understand how the other one feels. We were the same age when we lost our parents. Her mother's dead, too."

"I'm sorry to hear that, but don't you think it's a bit of a coincidence?"

"What do you mean?"

"That *both* of you lost *both* your parents when you were *both* the same age?" He paused, hoping the question would sink into his little brother's head. "Come on. You've got to admit that's quite a coincidence."

Silence. Then...

"You should have heard Wes. Should have heard what he said about her before he left. Then I discovered Megan overheard him. God, her face. It was terrible."

"Did she throw a tantrum like the redhead?"

"That's just it. She didn't. Stood as proud as can be with one adorable tear sliding down her face and told me she understood."

"Only *one* adorable tear?"

"Shut up, Will. It's not funny. She ran out, and I haven't heard from her since. She's even blocked my number."

"You do know that could be a ploy on her part don't you?"

Silence.

"Look, I know Wes can be an ass sometimes, but he has your best interests at heart. We both do."

"Why did I have to have two older brothers with such an interest in my affairs?"

"It could be a lot worse." Will chuckled. "You could have *three* older brothers who feel that way."

Chris burst out laughing. A good sign he wasn't totally heartbroken.

"That'll be the day," Chris said, referring to his twin, Cal, who was six minutes older.

"Look, give it a few weeks. If you still feel something for this girl, I'll meet her. But not right now. I'm with Wes on this, at least until we learn more about her."

"Okay. Fine. I'll see you soon."

"What time does your plane arrive?"

"I'm picking up Cal at the Miami airport, then we're driving. Remember?"

"Oh, that's right. Be careful." It was crazy for the three of them not to travel to the Keys together, but he understood Chris and Cal's need for their own wheels.

Will hit *end,* then punched in Wes's number. It rang three times and went to voicemail.

"Wes. Listen, bro, you need to leave Chris and his girlfriends to me. Your blunt, accusatory words are only making things worse. Your tactless charm may work on Cal, but not on Chris. The girl apparently heard you, and Chris is all up in arms about it. Call me."

He slid his phone back into his pocket. Hopefully, his brother got the message.

He grabbed the Jaguar door handle and heard the familiar click, signifying the car had unlocked at his touch. He turned right onto Tamiami Trail, then headed for Moorings Beach. Flowering oleanders and date palms disappeared in his line of vision along with Chris and his girlfriend troubles.

All the way there he played over in his mind the introduction to Miss Clare Sullivan.

Clare.

He liked her name.

Liked her stormy green eyes and her full pink lips.

He liked her dark shoulder-length hair, with its wispy bangs that framed her heart-shaped face to perfection.

He shook his head and glanced sideways out the window. *If Wes could hear me now, he'd have me committed.* God help him, if he didn't fully understand what Chris was going through. They were two of a kind. So much alike, *they* should have been twins.

He crossed Gulf Shore Boulevard and headed for home. Rubbing his chin, he thought of the many girls he'd been infatuated with when in high school and college. But in the end, none of them were right. He wanted to spare Chris this destructive path and knew in Wes's own blunt way, *he* did as well.

He sped past Amy's Chocolate Bar, then took the next right toward the beach. He wondered if his and Chris's misguided choices in women weren't a result of losing their parents. At times he felt he was looking for something, but it always seemed to elude him. He, of all people, knew that everyone reacted differently to the same event. One had only to look at the other two brothers to realize the truth of that. Wes and Cal were nothing like he and Chris. He and Chris tempered their words, were known to be good listeners, but Cal and Wes said whatever came into their heads, with little thought to whom it could hurt or to what circumstances it could affect. Straight and to the point, that was them.

The sun was low in the sky when he pulled into the driveway of his wood-framed beach cottage. He parked and got out. He mounted the steps, then threw open the side door that led to the narrow hallway near the kitchen. His brothers had scoffed at his choice of dwelling. Apparently, compact and comfortable was not suitable for a Carrington. He'd bought the penthouse in Miami, not to shut them up, but because of its family history. Another thing Wes would have ragged him about. His twin had no sentiment for anything old, family related or not. He'd no interest in his homes becoming museums.

The penthouse was old and in need of a complete overhaul, plus it had cost a small fortune. While Wes bought the most modern of homes, and the newest and best Miami and the Keys could offer, Will preferred the opposite. So when their grandparents' penthouse had come on the market, Will bought it immediately.

Neither Wes nor his younger brothers really understood his desire for the older more traditional architecture. He enjoyed researching his family history and often wished he'd had the forethought to ask their parents about their past when they were still alive.

Speaking of, he wondered if Carol had contacted *Miss Unhappy*. Thinking of her pretty pout, he smiled. It wasn't like any pout *he'd* ever seen. It said, *all business and hands off*.

A sudden, unwanted thought made him pause in the act of grabbing a sparkling water from the fridge. Had she wanted to meet him? He knew from Ken's surprised expression that they didn't have much of a past. Most in that position would have acknowledged each other with a nod of the head before getting on with their day. But not her.

He'd noticed her and the younger girl before she'd come over. Now that he thought about it, she'd practically shot from her chair. Shoulders back, head held high, she presented the very picture of regal authority as she approached their table.

She interrupted their conversation without a single bat of her lovely long lashes. Her eyes hadn't glazed cold until she'd looked right at him. *Damn.* Wondering what game she was playing, he took a swig of his water.

'Gold digger' flashed across his brain. No way. He knew from experience women after the Carrington fortune were all smiles. Clare Sullivan was well off. Picture perfect in her designer dress and heels. And apparently well established in her field. He'd heard good things about Lot's House Designs. They only hired the best. Nope, she was *not* interested in his money.

He'd have to call Ken and ply him for more details about her. But first, a walk on the beach. He kicked off his shoes, slipped out of his jacket, then headed out the door. Miss Sullivan's glowing, accusatory eyes came right along with him.

Chapter Two

Clare had been completely caught off guard by Will Carrington's secretary's call. Talk about out of the blue.

When she'd given him her card, she certainly hadn't expected him to follow up. Surely the man had access to the best design firms in South Florida, if not the entire state. Plus, his treatment of her sister galled her to no end.

She had no interest in meeting him again, or helping him. But if she was serious about giving up her share of the Pendelikon fortune, she needed to reconsider his offer. Would it be wise to forgo a lucrative assignment only because she didn't like someone?

She'd certainly worked with her share of unlikeable clients in the past. This would just be another such assignment. She'd been building up her client list since she'd left Lot's House, and the benefit of Carrington's referrals would be a major boost to her business.

She recovered her poise within a few short seconds, put on her professional self, and said she'd be happy to meet with him, but could not promise anything beyond that. She hung up. At least she'd have a week to think about it.

Spring break turned out to be one of the best she'd ever had with her sister. They ended up booking a suite at the Ritz in Naples with a room overlooking the Gulf of Mexico. They laughed, swam, and wiled away blissful hours in the sun. They ate fresh seafood every night, indulged in Florida's signature dessert, Key Lime Pie, then worked it off in the hotel gym and with long walks on the beach.

They ended their week with another relaxing massage, then drove home.

Sunday afternoon, Clare hugged Megan goodbye and stayed in the front of the condominium until Megan was out of sight.

"You're just like a worried mamma." Edward stood next to her watching the Corvette fade in the distance.

"Me? What about you? I saw you swipe that tear." She loved to tease him. Knew she shouldn't, but his formal ways had both endeared and entertained from the moment of their first meeting nearly twenty years ago. "You're a softie, and you and I both know it."

"If you say so." Back straight and with his usual, haughty presence, he ambled along the curved, floral-encased walkway to the entrance.

She strolled beside him and waited while he opened the door for her. She'd been tempted to run ahead and hold the door for him, but knew he'd be insulted.

"Edward?"

"Yes, miss?"

"What made you choose this profession?"

"The Mallorys have been in service for generations. I saw no reason not to continue in that vein. I'm no spring chicken, as you Americans like to say. This is all I've ever done. I worked for Mr. Fredrick Pendelikon before I came to work for his son. And will continue to serve this family for as long as you and Megan will have me."

"Quite noble of you. But you and I both know your continued and much-wanted presence was stipulated by my stepfather in his will."

"That is indeed true."

Clare knew the stipulation was as much for Edward's benefit, as it was for hers and Megan's. She also knew James Pendelikon had left Edward a sizable sum of his own. "Edward, both Megan and I want you to know we won't hold you to it if you should ever wish to go out on your own."

"As you frequently remind me, Miss Clare."

She laughed and looped her arm through his as they made their way across the lobby floor.

"Please know that I am not deaf." He patted her hand. "That I have heard you and appreciate your concern for my welfare." He cleared his throat. "May I be blunt?"

"Of course."

"The fact has not escaped me that for the past several months you've mentioned my welfare on more than one occasion. Several in fact. Do you wish me to leave?"

"No. Of course not. It's just...I may be going out on my own, and I wanted to make sure you would stay with Megan if I did so."

He raised a dark brow. "If I may be so bold, you have an odd way of going about securing that."

She chuckled. "You've succeeded in convincing me."

Edward pushed the button to the left of the elevator doors. "Are you planning on leaving soon?"

"Oh gosh, no. Megan has to finish college first. I wouldn't think of leaving before then."

"Good."

They stepped inside, turned, and stood side by side as the doors closed.

"And when I say leaving," Clare continued, "I mean finding my own place. Close by, of course."

"Of course." Edward pushed number six to take them to the top floor penthouse, then glanced upward to watch the numbers scroll by. "I may be speaking out of turn, but I knew your stepfather since he was a boy, and I know he loved you as his own."

If this is about the money—"

"How do you think Mr. Pendelikon would feel about your decision? Just something to think about."

The doors opened, and Edward disappeared to his own quarters as Clare stepped down the opposite hall to hers. She entered her room, then threw herself across the queen-size bed. Truthfully, that was about all she'd been thinking of lately. She let out a heartfelt sigh, then turned onto her side.

Tucking her hands underneath her right cheek, she stared at the wall. She thought about the last day she'd sailed the *Palm Pilot*. She'd noticed the crack in the mast as she'd brought her into dock, fully intending to alert her parents about it. But she and her friends had gone out for pizza afterward, then she'd gotten home late and went to bed. Caught up in her own little world, she hadn't given the mast another thought.

If only I'd said something...

Clare pressed her forehead against her arm and closed her eyes. She'd lived off her stepfather's billions long enough. By the time she'd finished college, her guilt in their demise had increased. She'd tried, without success, to live off her own income, discovering all too quickly how much it took to live in an adult world. But her discouragement didn't last long. At twenty-two, she was hired by Florida's premier design firm, Lot's House Designs, as their youngest designer.

At twenty-five, she'd received access to her inheritance. A remarkable sum, but she'd refused to touch it. That was over a year ago. She wasn't a fool and knew James Pendelikon would never want her to feel this way, but she couldn't help it. Guilt over her irresponsible behavior had ravaged her heart and mind far too long. Her parents should be here. Now. Alive. And would be if not for her. Her only penance was to finish raising Megan and get out on her own.

The meeting with Will Carrington was the following morning. She'd pretty much decided she'd listen to what he had to say, then politely inform him that she was *not* interested. After she told him off, of course.

CHAPTER THREE

Will pushed his cuff back and checked the time. 9:50. *She should be here any moment now.*

Carol opened his door. "Mr. Carrington. Miss Sullivan is here."

Will stepped from behind his cherry desk and shook Clare's hand. "Come on in."

She was wearing a white linen dress, sleeveless and cut high over her shoulders, accentuating her slender golden arms.

"Mr. Carrington."

She tipped her regal head toward him like a queen to her subject and placed her well-manicured hand in his, giv- ing it a brief, all-business squeeze, which he returned with pleasure.

"Please. Call me Will."

He led her to one of the four chairs in his office suite and sat across from her. As she took the seat, her hair swung appealingly across her bare shoulders, creating a fetching portrait. With the sun to her back, she sat poised and professional, unaware of the subtle red glow dancing off her dark hair.

He crossed his legs, folded his hands in his lap, and looked right at her.

After glancing around the room, she settled her green gaze on him.

Something about her direct look reminded him of his fourth grade teacher, Mrs. Mueller. Clare was far more beautiful, but her challenging eyes gave him the feeling he was in trouble.

"This is a wonderful space. Plenty of room and natural light. Whoever decorated it did a very nice job."

"Thank you. I think so, too."

"Why aren't you using her for your penthouse?"

"Actually, it was a *him*. Kevin Anderson. You may have heard of him."

"Yes. Everyone in my line of work knows who he is. I heard he and his wife moved to New York."

"That's right."

"Not so far away that someone with your means couldn't afford to continue to use him."

"I prefer to use local talent whenever I can. Or do you think someone with my *means,* incapable of such a feat?" Now why had he said that? Maybe there was more 'Wes' in him than he'd realized. But something about her reeked of snobbery. A trait he despised.

A rose-pink display marched slowly up her cheeks. Completely eradicating the acutely maintained ultra-professional calm she'd so beautifully displayed up until that moment. Her reaction was unexpected, and he wondered if he'd misjudged her haughty carriage for nervousness.

"I'm sorry if I offended you," she said.

Even with her slightly raised chin, her eyes held a note of regret.

"My own mother hired only the best," she added. "And if that meant flying them in from New York, London, or Paris, then she did."

"Don't worry. The job is still yours."

The remorse in her eyes vanished. "Excuse me? I don't recall you offering me a job, nor have I accepted one."

He pulled himself up short, not at all surprised at her annoyance. He'd pretty much asked for it.

"Now it seems I've offended *you*." The rise and fall of her breasts and the continued haughty angle of her lovely chin was a sure sign of it.

He had the sudden, strongest desire to get to know this woman. He gazed into her smoldering eyes. If he'd learned anything from his past where women were concerned, he should be able to recognize a genuine response of having been offended or some fake nonsense. For the life of him, he couldn't tell in her case. However, he was certain of one thing. She did *not* like him and that fascinated him.

"My apologies, but your earlier comment rubbed me the wrong way. If I misunderstood, then please forgive *me*. How about we start again?"

His cell phone rang. He took it from his pocket to turn the ringer off, and saw it was from Wes. Talk about poor timing. He wasn't sure when Wes was leaving for Puerto Rico, so he needed to take this. "Excuse me, I'll just be a minute."

He stood up and crossed to the other side of the suite. "Hey, I need to call you back."

Clare had gotten up and was perusing his bookcase. He watched her pull out his books on sailing, then turned away to speak with his brother.

"So. You heard about Chris's latest little gold digger?" Wes said.

"Yes, I heard about his latest gold digger, and that's exactly what I want to talk to you about, but not right now."

"I've got to hand it to him, this one certainly is a cute little thing."

Will glanced back over his shoulder. Clare stood ramrod straight, her hand stilled over the book. He turned his attention back to Wes. "I see you got a good look at her." He hoped his sarcasm wasn't lost on his brother.

"I sure did. I sat in the car and watched them cuddle like two love birds on the porch before she went inside the frat house."

"You spied on her?" He lowered his voice. He could only imagine Wes's grin on the other end of the line. "One of these days," he whispered, "your interference is going to backfire."

He found it hard to believe he and Wes were brothers, much less identical twins. Except for their looks, there was nothing identical about them.

"Look, I have to go," Will said.

"Okay. Call me when you're free." Wes rung off.

Will walked back over to Clare who was seated again and flipping through the book. Was it his imagination or was something wrong? Her entire countenance had hardened. Her eyes were glacial as she stared at the page in front of her.

"Do you like to sail?" he asked.

"I used to."

Stilted and formal, she closed the book with a snap.

He blinked.

She raised her head and looked right at him. The epitome of poise and perfection, with a slight smile on her lips that clearly said she knew something he didn't. It didn't bode well for him, he was certain. There was a time in his greener days when a pair of accusing eyes and a mysterious smirk threatened. Instinct told him to let her go right then and there. But the fire in her eyes issued the ultimate dare that all but demanded a response.

"So, are you interested in working with me?"

Her smile grew, but her eyes still held no joy. Nothing that mirrored the pleasant, if not *sudden*, tilt of her full lips.

The feeling hit him again. She didn't like him.

At.

All.

What the heck had he done to her? He took in her expensive clothes and high heels. The phrase, *dressed to kill,* popped into his brain. His mind raced over his past life and the scorned women in it. To a time when he did most of his thinking with the body part south of his head and heart. There were only two, but could she be a sister to one of them? Out for revenge? He tugged at the collar of his shirt.

If that were the case, then he'd gladly accept the challenge. Each one of those women deserved the swift kick he'd given to their delightful bottoms. He had zero respect for a woman who'd secure a man's heart purely for financial gain.

"Why, I'd love nothing better than to work with you." She crossed her long, leggy limbs, then leaned back and propped her elbows along the sides of the chair with a graceful flourish he found fascinating. "When would you like to begin?"

Said the spider to the fly.

A combination of excitement and trepidation coursed through his veins. "The sooner the better," he said.

Chapter Four

Clare had arrived at Will's office with every intention of discussing his accusations regarding Megan. Calmly and rationally, like adults. She'd hoped to clear up any misunderstanding on his part. Assure him her sister had no need for Carrington money. But his gold digger comment rang in her ears like a clanging bell.

Gold digger.

Gold digger.

Cling. Clang. Clong.

She'd work with him all right. Work him over, that is. Charge him a fortune, then put the money in her savings. And when she was through, he'd rue the day he ever hurt her sister.

They'd planned to meet back at his office in two days. He insisted they fly to Miami together where they could go over the floor plans, then she could see the apartment.

She arrived bright and early on the designated day. After entering his office building, she sat down on a leather bench near a huge Ficus tree and waited.

When he stepped off the elevator, she rose to meet him.

"Good morning. You're very prompt, Clare." His eyes mirrored admiration as he took in her yellow dress.

"Good morning."

Stiff and formal. Good. The more they kept to the niceties, the better. Although, she had the nagging feeling he had just mocked her.

"My car's waiting out front. Come on."

She followed along beside him into the bright Florida sunshine. He held the door of his champagne-colored Jag while she climbed inside. He sat in the back next to her and motioned for his driver to go.

They arrived at Naples Municipal Airport and got out.

"We're not taking a commercial flight?"

"I only fly commercial when I go overseas." He spread his arm toward an executive jet. "Your carriage awaits, my lady." His firm lips broke into a smile that threatened to upset her equilibrium.

Yes, he was mocking her. She knew she came across somewhat stiff and formal. A habit she'd acquired after working with several wealthy high-powered clients from New York. She found it most useful in keeping her usual expressive self at bay. It was especially handy when dealing with clients she didn't like.

The aircraft was a Pendelikon P500. One of her stepfather's. Sadly, he'd died before this particular model was finished. Her gaze devoured the sleek lines of the body. Their estate owned two such aircrafts, very similar in design. Her stepfather believed one should always be in reserve in case the other one had to be grounded. James Pendelikon believed in efficiency and order. And never left anything to chance nor allowed for delay or interruption to any of his plans, if he could help it.

But with all of his experience, he and her mother had still drowned. A raw ache penetrated her heart. She shook the uncomfortable feeling off and continued across the tarmac to the waiting plane.

"You're not nervous are you?"

Clare could see concern in his eyes. That surprised her. She had better watch her moments of sadness. Will Carrington was far too perceptive.

"No. I was just thinking of something else. Sorry."

She hoped that would stop any further comment or, heaven forbid, more questions.

They mounted the steps and boarded the plane. She was hit with the familiar smell of handcrafted leather and freshly brewed coffee. She couldn't help but think of her parents and the last vacation they'd all taken together. They'd flown to the Bahamas where they sailed around the islands, snorkeled, and fished. They'd played and ate, then played some more. It was a happy, blissful escape.

She settled in one of the recliner seats in the middle of the cabin.

"Would you like a snack or something to drink?" he said.

She'd noticed he'd had their short flight catered. The selection of finger sandwiches and tiny frosted cakes looked delicious. "I'll have a Perrier with a dash of orange juice, if it's not too much trouble."

The plane started to taxi as he mixed their drinks. He handed her the juice spritzer, then sat down and buckled his seat belt.

She glanced out the side window, sipping the icy drink. The smooth liftoff always thrilled and had her heart thudding. She loved flying and knew it was because she was spoiled. She'd probably hate it if she had to stand in long lines at the airport and suffer the hassles most travelers had to endure just to get through security.

"This is nice." She looked at her companion who was studying her. She smiled and took another sip of her drink.

"It is, isn't it? I feel fortunate every time I'm in this jet. It's beautiful, comfortable, and safe. Pendelikon has some of the best engineers in the industry. I wouldn't own anything else."

She nodded, keeping her gaze on him as he spoke. It was nice to know he appreciated *something* about the Pendelikons.

"Have you ever flown in a business jet?"

Not keen on lying, she'd have to be careful here. She couldn't let on how much she knew about this model.

"I've had the pleasure. It was an older model than this, but still very nice."

It was a year ago. She and her sister had taken their jet to the West Coast to look at colleges during Megan's spring break.

He raised a dark eyebrow. "Well, heck. I was hoping I was treating you to your first small jet experience."

She lifted her glass in salute. "Well, there are other first time experiences. Maybe you and I can share in something else before my job is completed." She gave him a sparkling smile, hoping to change the subject away from airplanes.

"What does your father do?"

So much for stilling the questions. Since she'd never known her real father and since both were gone, she decided to go with her stepdad. "He and my mother are deceased."

"I'm so sorry."

"It's okay. It happened years ago."

"My parents are gone, too. It can be tough. Especially when you're young."

She nodded and sipped from her glass.

"What was your father's line of work?"

She licked her lips. "He started out as a mechanic."

"Cars?"

She cleared her throat. "Airplanes."

He suddenly seemed more alert. Like a kid in a candy store, his interest soared as he swiveled his chair toward her.

"Did he work on commercial jobs? Like Boeing or Pendelikon?"

Clare almost spewed her juice from her lips. She swallowed and glanced at his animated face. *My gosh. He really is interested.*

"Yes. He started out on the big planes, but later his interest in the smaller jets drew him." She hoped that was enough to satisfy. It would be so easy to spill everything about her stepfather, his interests, his family money, which allowed him to invest in his own line of commercial and business jets. Guilt washed over her as she thought about his energy and life.

"Are you okay?"

She nodded and turned away, quickly blinking away the tears that suddenly threatened.

"It must be difficult taking about your father."

"No, but sometimes when I least expect it, I'm overcome. I apologize. I never cry in front of strangers. Especially in front of clients. You must think me–"

"Not at all," he said. "My father passed away years ago, and my mother in recent years. Not a day goes by that I don't think of one or both of them. Sometimes it can be the most insignificant thing that brings them to my thoughts."

For a brief moment, his face clouded over, then it was gone. He stood and stepped over to the serving area.

She gazed out the window, taking in the breathtaking view of blue sky and puffy white clouds. Will Carrington wasn't as bad as she'd thought. Especially if his complimentary remarks regarding Pendelikon aircraft were sincere.

She thought of her mom and dad and smiled, knowing they'd both find her position humorous. The verdict was still out, though, and she had a score to settle. She had no idea when or how, but the situation was starting to be fun. And that was something she hadn't experienced in a long, long time.

* * *

Will fixed himself a gin and tonic. More to kill time than anything else. So her father died years ago just like his. *How convenient.*

Earlier, he'd rejected the idea she could be after his money. Everything about her pointed to wealth and success. But just because she was well off, didn't mean she wasn't out for more.

Had he slighted her in some way? Was it possible she could be using the same ploy on him as that college girl had pulled on Chris? He took a sip of his drink, then another. And here he was babbling on about his deceased parents like he'd known her for years. Man she was good. He sounded as green as ever.

He cut his eyes in her direction. She was gazing out the window, deep in thought, swirling the short straw through the ice in her empty glass. Her eyes sparkled like gems. She looked happy. Content. Did she think she'd scored? The corners of her mouth lifted. His chest tightened. *Damn.* Happiness looked good on her.

He sucked in a deep breath, then swallowed. He'd have to figure out a way to let her go. A man in his position could not get embroiled with some spite-driven female. After they toured the condo, he'd wait twenty-four hours, then inform her he'd decided to use someone else.

Or, he could keep her on the project, watch, wait, and get to know her, and *if* what he suspected was true, then he'd turn the tables and catch her for the revenge-seeking, money grubber she really was. And if not, then he would've accomplished his design goals for the penthouse and enjoyed the company of a beautiful woman. Either way it was a win-win.

"How about a refill?"

She turned her attention to his and smiled, this time it reached her eyes. In that moment, she was beautiful. *Radiant.* Whatever the result, getting to know Miss Sullivan would hopefully have its own reward.

"Sure. And I'd love one of those little sandwiches and cakes."

Will viewed this sudden change in her demeanor more like a warning than actual proof that she was up to something. Only time would tell. He wasn't a college freshman anymore. He was the co-owner of one of the most successful coffee plantations in the world. This leggy, all-business designer was a challenge he would enjoy taking on, whatever the result.

In his younger days, he'd learned the hard way about women. Especially after several near deaths at their sticky fingers, scheming smiles, and swaying hips. Could he possibly have missed seeing it in *her*? There was no doubt something was *off* here, but what?

Their eyes met as he passed her the drink. If this was a game, he'd personally make sure it wasn't all one-sided. That just wouldn't be fair.

Chapter Five

A sleek limo was waiting for them when they landed. Will handed his briefcase to the driver, then held the door as she got in.

"The condo's only a few minutes from here," he said. "I thought we'd do a walk-through first, then have lunch and discuss your ideas."

"Sounds good." She nodded. "Anything you want to tell me about your lifestyle?"

He raised a cocky well-groomed brow at her.

"It helps me when forming a plan for my clients. It's not just a home I'm decorating, but a way of life for the one who lives there."

"Of course. Let's see..." He cleared his throat. "At first, I had no interest in buying another place, but my brothers insisted on it. I frankly had no interest until this particular property came on the market, so I bought it. More out of obligation, and honestly, I haven't given much thought on how I plan to use it. Any suggestions?" He smiled, and her heart thudded in her chest.

"So you bought it just to please someone else?"

"Basically. And because—"

"Why would you do that? You obviously have wealth, so why not do as you please?"

"Is that what you think? Because one has wealth, one does what they please? If so, you have a poor view of the wealthy."

Not the wealthy, just the Carringtons.

His lips formed a thin line as his eyes bored into hers. She lowered her gaze. *Watch it. You'll be getting yourself fired if you're not careful.*

"I'm sorry." She forced herself to look at him. "I have a habit of speaking my mind. That was an ugly, judgmental comment."

"Based on past experience?"

Her heart stuttered as she looked straight at him. His intense gaze held a question, but she got the impression it was completely different from the one he'd just asked. "Something like that," she said.

He nodded. "I understand. I've been fortunate when it comes to my portfolio, but please know I would not take kindly to fools who assume I didn't work long and hard for every penny I have."

Great. He thinks I'm a fool. "Look, I just think it's a bit crazy to buy a house you may not want just to please someone else. That's the only point I was trying to make." She gave him her most sincere expression and sighed. When he didn't respond further, she continued. "So you're a self-made man."

"Not entirely. But, I, along with my brother, have worked years to further develop the family business started by our great-grandfather."

"Then you're to be commended."

They turned onto a wide boulevard marking the entrance to the 1920's condominium. Clare caught her breath. The red tile roof and stucco building still held the charm and character of when it was built. It was clear that whoever owned the building had certainly maintained the integrity of the original structure. Joy skipped over her heart and like a giddy kid, she leaned out of the car window and looked up. Royal Palms flanked the wide entryway to the building and heralded their approach like royalty.

Once inside, Will inserted a brass key in the side panel of the elevator and unlocked the door. They entered a private elevator, which took them directly to the penthouse foyer.

The doors opened to an Art Deco dream. The wide, marble-floored foyer greeted her like an old friend. As she crossed into the main living area, all her angst against the man walking beside her faded. Beautiful high-ceilinged arms engulfed her in all their vintage glory, from the intricate detail of the crown molding to the warm patina of the hardwood floors. So many of the condos were new and way too modern for her tastes. But to get her hands on a jewel like this was a dream come true.

* * *

"This is amazing." Clare let out a breathless squeak. Delight lit her face in a way Will hadn't yet seen. He was pleased she liked the condo, but still highly suspicious of her motives. This woman was certainly an enigma. One moment she seemed to despise him and the next she was a giddy schoolgirl who'd just been asked to the prom.

"I'll take your awed expression as a good sign," he said.

"It's remarkable. In perfect condition. Truly lovely." She threw her hands over the area, turning slowly in the center of the main room.

"Yes, it is. I know it needs a great deal of work, but my real estate agent told me it would bring a fortune if I ever decided to sell." Not that he'd sell anytime soon.

"Oh, don't ever sell it." She shook her head and stepped toward the long bank of windows overlooking the ocean. "I've dreamed of owning a place like this for years."

He followed her to the windows. "And the view?" He knew her answer before she uttered a word.

"Breathtaking."

The Atlantic Ocean spanned miles before them. The water glistened in the sunlight, beckoning with its mesmerizing dance.

"The other day in the office, you told me you used to sail."

Her glowing expression suddenly sobered. Intrigued, he watched her closely.

"I...yes. But, I haven't in a long time."

He took note of her hesitation and wondered if something unfortunate had happened.

"Maybe before you're finished here, we can remedy that." She'd poured over his sailing book in his office a week ago. It was clear she loved sailing or at least the romance of it. When she hadn't known he'd been watching, she'd gazed at the pages like a lost lover, turning them almost reverently.

The slight smile that played about her mouth had captured his interest even then. He'd wondered what it would be like to kiss those glossy pink lips. He focused on them now, and knew in spite of his unanswered questions he'd still love nothing more than to place his mouth against hers.

"I'll need to know your budget for the project?" She interrupted his musings.

"Money's no problem."

"Great. We can come up with a firmer figure after I get more information." She took a turn about the roomy space. "Your office is quite modern. Are you thinking along those same lines for this place?"

"I'm not much on clutter. I tend to go for the cleaner look." He shrugged. "What do you think?"

"I agree. You don't want to clutter such a beautiful place. You want the architectural bones to breathe, if you know what I mean."

"I think I do."

She lovingly ran her fingers along the ornate chair rail in the dining area, then stepped back, covered her heart with her hands, and gazed upward toward the crown molding. "The architectural features alone can work as art. Add a few period pieces amongst some transitional ones and you can have yourself quite a showplace. Beautiful *and* comfortable."

Continuing to soak up every detail, she walked back to the center of the large living room. "On a project of this magnitude, I usually like to spend time with the client." She stopped in her perusal and turned toward him. "It helps to know your interests, what you like, your personal tastes. You know, in color, design, and style. That sort of thing. I'm sure you're busy. Will that be a problem?"

"Not at all. I like the sound of spending time with you."

Her pretty mouth dropped open. Uncertainty clouded her green gaze. *Good.* He'd thrown her for a loop. She needed to be kept on her toes. He glanced at her feet. Or at least on her open-toed high heels.

"Um, sure." She blinked as if willing herself back to the present. "I'm just finishing up with a couple of clients and can give you my full attention next week. How does that sound?"

Earlier, he'd planned to fire her before they ever got started. But the sparkle in her countenance as she floated from room to room and her passion and enthusiasm for her work and his home mesmerized him.

Since that first meeting, he'd been attracted to her. In the days that followed, he could think of little else but seeing her again. Truthfully, he wanted her to be the real deal, and the only way to find out was to spend time with her. Something wasn't right, and damn if that didn't add to the hunt. Plus, he hadn't been this excited to get to know a woman since sophomore, Penelope Snyder, accosted him between the open stacks in Florida State's library.

* * *

Will had a meeting that afternoon, so Clare spent the time visiting some of her favorite antique shops in the area. They arranged to meet a couple of hours later. After putting a few small items on hold, she spotted Will just outside the shop.

"Hey, I thought that was you." Will pushed through the door and sauntered over to her side.

"Hi there. You're early. I've barely even started in here."

"We finished earlier than I'd expected. I tried to call, but you didn't answer."

"Sorry, I had to silence my phone in the last shop I was in." She slipped it from her purse and turned it back on.

"I spotted you inside so I thought I'd join you before we fly back." He gazed around the store. "This place is something else. You have excellent taste, Clare."

"Thank you."

"Do you need to continue shopping or do we have time for a cup of coffee before we head back? There's a fabulous little Cuban place around the corner. They have the best pastries."

"Sure. We can do that, but let's take a few minutes and walk through here together. This would be a good time to show me what you like."

They strolled through the congested shop, picking up objects and checking the prices.

"How do you do it?" he said.

"Do what?"

"Siphon through all this junk. There's stuff everywhere. I'm beginning to feel claustrophobic."

"Some of this *junk* costs a pretty penny." She stopped in front of a table loaded with lamps. "This one's nice." Clare pointed to a brass, figurine lamp. "Shall I put it on hold?"

A frown formed between his eyes, and he shook his head. "You like that?"

She didn't, but it was a perfect 1920's era piece. He scrunched up his nose as she picked up another lamp to check the price. She found herself enjoying the moment. Something about this self-assured man resurrected her mischievous streak. A streak she'd buried along with her parents.

She loved that she knew something about him that he didn't. Loved she had a secret in regard to him, her sister and his younger brother. That gave her an edge he didn't have over her.

She gazed around the shop, mentally choosing a few tacky objects and wondered what it would be like to use such painfully, awful stuff in his beautiful condo. At that moment, her most recent decorating nightmare, Laney, and her penchant for everything gold came to mind. Picturing his reaction, she toyed with the idea of taking a few tips from the woman. Then a little voice whispered in her ear, reminding her about Megan's hurt feelings. Something she'd forgotten about in the magical tour of his penthouse and their current pleasantries. His forehead still creased with dislike at the garish items surrounding them.

As she gazed at him, she played a few scenarios in her mind. It would be such fun to disarm this man. Her heart hummed a ditty. She hadn't felt this carefree in years. An unexpected tear rushed to one eye and she blinked it away. Welcome back, *Clare Girl.*

Thirty minutes later, they entered the coffee shop and got in line. The place was only half-full so there were plenty of tables.

"Can I trust you?"

Clare's mouth suddenly went dry. "What?"

A teasing twinkle lit his eyes, and his lips quirked at the corners. "I said, can I trust you?" He glanced meaningfully at the pastry shelves lined up in front of them. "To order for me. I have to make a quick phone call." He slid his iPhone from his pocket, then waved it in front of her.

"Oh, sure. Of course," she said. "What would you like?"

"You choose. And when I get back, I'll see if your excellent taste extends to the culinary world."

He stepped outside, and Clare slowly let out a breath. She watched him punch in a number, then place the phone to his ear. His expression took on a serious note. She wished she could hear what he was saying and wondered fleetingly if it concerned Megan and Chris.

She turned away and perused the assortment of pastries stacked in neat rows behind the curved glass.

"May I help you?" A short, dark-haired girl stood patiently behind the counter, beaming a bright smile.

"Hi. Yes. This is the first time I've been here. Everything looks fabulous. What do you suggest?"

"It's all good, but I like the key lime pie and if you like chocolate, the flourless chocolate cake is to die for."

"Great. I'll take one of each."

Will returned just as the server handed Clare the desserts and coffee.

"I've got this," he said.

She nodded and carried the tray to a booth at the farthest window and sat down.

After Will paid, he joined her in the booth, sliding in opposite her. "This looks great. The chocolate is for me, right?"

She'd just forked a generous bite of the chocolate delicacy, then gaped at him. "In your dreams."

"Admit it." He chuckled. "You thought I was serious. But don't worry. If there's anything I know, it's that women and chocolate go together."

"That's rather sexist, isn't it? Especially, since you *really* want it." She popped the decadent morsel between her lips and blatantly locked eyes with his.

"It's the truth, and you know it. And sweetheart, you just demonstrated it beautifully."

"Seriously?"

"Okay, fine. You take the pie."

As he reached for the chocolate cake, she snatched it out of his reach, then slid an ample amount of the creamy confection into her mouth.

He laughed. A rich, masculine sound that set off an inner spark. Dang he was attractive. If she weren't careful, his charm would have her slipping into his seductive world.

She paused in her chewing and stared at him. His eyes crinkled at the corners, and the twinkle in their depths made her heart pound. No man had ever made her feel the way he was at this moment. He was quite remarkable, and she realized she'd better be careful. It wouldn't do to lose her heart to a scoundrel.

She snatched up her napkin and dabbed her mouth. Something, *anything* to break that mesmerizing smile of his. Not the best distraction, but better than sitting there staring. Then, summoning up the Pendelikon poise, she straightened her back and primly took another bite. She needed to focus on something other than Will Carrington's charm.

* * *

"So, tell me what you do all day?" Clare dabbed a napkin to her lips.

"Back to business, already? I thought we could at least finish dessert."

"Now's as good a time as any to find out more about you." She placed the fork on the table, sat back against the vinyl booth, then removed a small, spiral notebook and pen from her purse. She looked expectantly at him.

Miss Haughty returns. He must confess he still had trouble trusting her motives. Earlier, when he'd asked her if he could trust her, her startled, wide-eyed, response was palpable. He was simply referring to dessert, but her reaction pointed to something more.

"Let's see." He sliced his fork into the pie. "I get up in the morning, I have coffee. I take a shower, then I get dressed. I drive to the office, then check the stock market."

She stopped writing and raised her perfectly plucked brows at him. "That's not exactly the type of information I was looking for."

"You wanted to know what I did all day. I assumed you wanted details."

She pursed her lips and sucked in a slow deep breath. "Look, I know you go to your office. You undoubtedly have meetings."

"Undoubtedly."

She huffed out a breath. "And, I *assume* as a business-man, you travel on occasion."

"You see? You already know what I do all day."

She snapped the tablet shut. "You're right. You business-men are all alike." Just as she went to jam it inside her purse, he grabbed her hand.

"I'm sorry. I'll behave. But on one condition."

"Which is?"

"You pass me the rest of your chocolate cake."

She sighed and pushed the plate across the table.

"Now may we continue?" she said.

"Absolutely." He dove into the rich dessert, or what was *left* of it.

Flipping the tablet back open, she continued. "What are your outside interests? What do you do for fun?"

"I like water sports. Sailing, scuba diving, fishing. Aren't you going to write that down?"

She put the pen to the paper. "Enjoys outdoor activities."

"Water sports," he purposely clarified.

"Anything else?"

"I like to read. Biographies, mainly."

"Enjoys learning about other people." She scribbled across the page as she spoke out loud.

"Is it necessary to repeat everything I say?"

She raised her eyes and looked at him. "I'm sorry. Do my stilted, boring answers bother you?"

"Touché."

"I think..." She snapped the tablet shut and stuffed it in her purse along with the pen. "I have enough information to get started. You know. If we're going to be working together, it would be helpful if—"

"Why did you take this job?"

She stiffened, touched her throat, opened her mouth as if she was going to speak, then clamped her lips together. For a split second, her gaze lowered to her purse, then she glanced back up. "It's my work. I had an opening, and I love what I do."

"True. But, I get the feeling you don't like me." There, it was out. But would she take the bait and be honest with him?

She stared at him, the slight widening of her eyes giving the only hint he'd surprised her. "I'm sorry you've gotten that impression." She sat fiddling with the handle of her purse, then paused as if to choose her words carefully. She clamped her teeth over her lower lip. "This is terribly em-barrassing."

She fluttered her lashes and low and behold if she didn't gaze adorably at him. Feminine wiles, this early in the day, too.

"I'm not even quite sure how to say it without sounding egotistical," she said.

He propped his elbows on the table and placed his chin in his hand. "I'm sure I can handle it."

"Well." She swallowed. "It wouldn't be the first time one of my clients got the wrong idea about my many questions. You see. Most of the time, they're quite personal, and I didn't want to give you the wrong idea."

"Heaven forbid."

"So, I tried to keep them short and general in nature."

"Let me make sure I understand. You're a beautiful woman and because of that men tend to misunderstand your motive behind all the personal questions? Is that it?"

He so enjoyed the pink flush that crept up her cheeks.

"That's not exactly what I meant, but it's close enough." She squirmed.

"Let me assure you. Your questions are welcome. You can be as irritating, intrusive, and personal as you'd like. I promise it won't bother me. Not one little bit. You can save your stiff, formal, nose-in-the-air attitude for someone else. And if it makes you feel any better, the last thing I intend is for your beautiful self to interest me in the slightest. And you can be certain your long legs have completely escaped my notice." He smiled his most engaging smile, never once taking his eyes off her uncomfortable face.

Merriment lit her eyes. Her lips quirked into a maddeningly cute grin. "I told you it would sound egotistical."

"Look. I can see you're a beautiful woman. I'm not blind. And I'm sure you've had your share of unfortunate run-ins with the male species. But I'm a professional, Miss Sullivan. Not a wolf. And until you say otherwise, our relationship will be completely platonic." He leaned back and draped his arms across the back of the booth. "So, ask away."

CHAPTER SIX

Until I say otherwise? Was he serious? Did he just say what I think he said? Why of all the arrogant...like I would ever come groveling at his feet for his romantic attention.

A knot formed in the pit of Clare's stomach. She took a hasty sip of water and fought for control, then set the glass down before she hurled it at his smug face. His unfair remarks regarding Megan suddenly came to the forefront, reminding her to get in, decorate, charge him a fortune, and get out.

Stick to the plan, Clare Girl.

She could not let on how badly he irritated her. She'd better put her angst aside regarding Megan, too, because this savvy coffee tycoon would take every pleasure in firing her.

Clutching her purse, she slid from the seat and stood. "I think I have everything I need for now." She glanced at her watch. "We really must get going."

After they landed in Naples, they took the limo back to his office.

"Thanks again for the tour and the dessert," she said. "I'll call you when I have something to show you."

"I'll be waiting." Will held her car door while she slid in.

Heat infused her entire body. She started the Prius and put the air on high.

She could kick herself for opening such a stupid topic. It was all she'd thought about on the flight home.

Really Clare? To insinuate Will Carrington would have the hots for you because of your personal questions? You are such an idiot.

She flicked on the blinker, checked her side mirror, and merged into the evening traffic. Will Carrington rattled her equilibrium, no doubt about that. She'd have to perform better in the future. And stop acting like some silly school-girl, too.

But all she could think about was his treatment of Megan and his dang good looks. No one that hateful should look so gorgeous. It simply wasn't fair. She'd have to ask better questions as well. The only reason she hadn't was because in his case it didn't matter. She already knew every-thing she wanted to know about the man. Arrogant, accusatory, unfair, and completely and utterly full of him-self.

She'd have to put personal feelings aside if this was go-ing to work. He was well known and highly regarded in the state and would be an asset to her resume. But if he fired her, it could ruin her career.

It was late when she pulled into the parking garage, but not so late that she didn't notice Megan's Corvette. The double beep assured her the Prius was locked as she continued on to the elevator.

Edward met her at the entrance and reached for her briefcase.

"Seriously, Edward. You really must get a life. This is not Downton Abbey." She tossed her handbag and sample case onto the foyer table.

Edward smiled, retrieved her case, and carried it to her office.

"You don't have to do that." Her words fell on deaf ears. Edward was across the wide foyer within seconds, ignoring her as always. "I have got to find him a wife," she mumbled, heading for the kitchen.

Yanking open the fridge she paused, staring into the brightly lit box of shelves. She chewed the inside of her cheek and grabbed a Perrier, unscrewed the top, then took a swig.

"You look like you need something a bit stronger." Megan stood inside the doorway holding a glass of white wine.

"You're not legal yet." Clare took the stemmed glass from Megan's fingers and tossed the remaining liquid down the sink.

"Hey, quit being so bossy. I'm at home. It's okay."

"It's not okay and I am *not* bossy."

Megan shot her a cheeky grin, then turned and flitted down the hall to the media room. "You know you are!" she yelled over her shoulder.

Clare blinked. "Hey, not so fast." She caught up with Megan just as she entered the room. "I know no such thing."

"You *are* bossy. Have been since Mom and Dad died. You used to be so much fun." She plopped onto the over-stuffed sofa sectional, propping her feet onto the coffee table. "Oh, don't look so stricken." She patted the seat beside her. "Here. Sit. You look terrible. Tell me about your day."

"You're such a brat." She took a long swig from the Perrier, then sat next to her sister.

"I know." Megan laughed. "And if you drank something stronger than sparkling water, you'd feel a lot better. So. Tell me? You working with a new client?"

"I am." She had to be careful. She didn't want Megan to know who she was working for.

"Who is it?"

"Oh, just some uppity businessman from Miami. You know the type. Thinking they own the world and every-thing in it."

"Which means thinking they know more than you."

"You got it." Clare needed to end this conversation—fast. "Okay. Spill. What are you doing here?"

Megan lifted her brows. "What? A girl can't come home?"

"You just left a week ago."

"And it's the weekend, and I wanted to come home."

"Is it Chris? Did something else happen with that brother of his?"

"It's Delta Gamma's spring fling. I was expecting to go with Chris." She shrugged. "It was too late to get another date, so I came home."

Clare looped her arm through Megan's. "I'm sorry." Megan was well liked by her peers, and Clare knew she'd have had no trouble getting another date. Which meant she must really be smitten with Chris. Another mark against Will Carrington.

After Megan went to bed, Clare felt restless. Someone should teach Carrington a lesson; too bad she didn't have the nerve.

Clare Girl would do it. Yeah. In the same way you made a fool out of me today.

But that didn't mean she couldn't have fun fantasizing about it. Megan was right about one thing. Clare used to be fun, but she'd laid her impish, playful streak aside after her parents had passed away. That was not an example for her sister to follow.

But, something about Will Carrington brought out *Clare Girl*. She had to admit, she liked that about him. He made her feel alive, like her old self. For the first time in years she took stock of her existence. How long was she planning to punish herself? What if it had been Megan instead of her? She'd never want her sister to suffer this kind of guilt.

She could hear her stepdad's voice now. Right in the middle of one of her mom's reprimands over Clare's latest prank with her friends. He'd wink and say, "That's my Clare Girl."

After brushing her teeth, she slipped on her nightgown, then curled up in bed with her laptop as an idea formed in her mind. The image of Carrington's disgust over some of the more ornate objects brought a smile to her lips.

She typed, 'gold digger - definition' in the search bar.

"A person who dates others purely to extract money from them."

She slumped back against the headboard. She supposed a wealthy, good-looking man had to be careful. She really did understand that some women were only interested in money and the things it could buy. She had absolutely no respect for anyone, woman or not, who used another for their own gain. But, that was not her sister. Frankly, it galled her to know Carrington not only thought it, but also acted on it as fact. She wondered again if she were doing the right thing working for him.

Since her parents' death, Clare had protected her sister as only a teenage girl could. She sighed. She hated that life had to change and get more complicated. It was so much easier when they were younger.

The Pendelikon fortune had provided well for them, with Edward's help, of course. Except for a few close school friends, they had no one. There were no aunts or uncles. No cousins. Maids, cooks, and nannies had filled the vacuum left by their parents' death. A sad substitute, but there it was.

She continued her search of the word *gold* and anything associated with it.

"Gold panning supplies. Here we go." A list of gold panning supplies along with photos filled the screen. "Here's something interesting. A sluice box. What the heck is that?"

"Who are you talking to?"

Clare swung around. Megan stood in the doorway in her nightshirt. "Oh. You know me. A regular ol' Chatty Kathy when I get excited about something."

"Yeah. Right." Megan rolled her eyes and left.

Clare turned her attention back to her laptop. She'd had no idea gold digging was such a science. It would be a fun theme party to implement. Someday.

She bookmarked several interesting sites to show Megan. If nothing else, they'd at least have a bit of fun with it.

She snapped her MAC shut, set it on the bedside table, then switched off the light. She snuggled deep into her down pillow and allowed her imagination to run free. Imagined the look on Will's face as he entered the condo to a flurry of pickaxes, pup tents, and gold panning gear. Imagined the charming Carrington smile vanishing from his arrogant face. It would serve him right for his treatment of her sister.

The next day, Clare sat at her worktable with the penthouse floor plans spread before her. She did a tentative sketch of where the furniture would go, making a note to get his thoughts before drawing a more detailed and to-scale plan.

Time for a break. She leaned back in her desk chair, stretching her arms over her head. That morning, she'd awakened with a clear vision of how she could decorate a place as a gold mining camp. She hadn't planned a theme party in a long time and the inspiration for a gold rush filled her brain.

She pulled out a blank sheet of drafting paper. Now was as good a time as any to jot down her ideas. She sketched a rustic workbench in the entry hall, then added a pickaxe across the top left corner. She drew an old-fashioned oil lamp to the right, then a few sticks of dynamite on a silver tray in the center. It was all rustic and displayed the kind of things one would find at an old mining camp. A gleeful rush of satisfaction soared as she looked at her work.

When she was through with the rendition, the penthouse housed everything from pickaxes and lanterns to mining tents and dynamite crates. She made a note to search for posters of scantily clad saloon girls in low-cut dresses. That and some other odds and ends about gold mining in general could be added later.

She stepped back to gain perspective over her work before sliding the sketch into an over-sized brown folder. For a moment, she paused and tried to imagine the design in Will's 1920's dream. She chewed her bottom lip. She'd never have the nerve to do it. Safety Susie. Control Freak Connie. She'd heard them all. She'd been called those and more since she'd taken on the role of mother and father to Megan. She'd had to grow up fast, and she'd never looked back. Megan was her responsibility, and that was that.

She'd just set the folder down when Megan popped her head through the doorway. "What's for breakfast?"

"Breakfast? It's almost lunchtime."

"Oh, can I see?" Megan sauntered over to Clare's worktable as Clare angled the Carrington design around for a better view.

"Wow. That looks great."

"Thanks. It's pretty basic right now. I'll add more details, of course, after I meet with my client." She hadn't told Megan who she was working for and wasn't quite sure if she should. It was obvious Megan was still hurt over

Will's comments to Chris. Plus, Clare didn't want Megan to influence her at this point in the game.

She paused. Was it a game? Yes. It was and the sooner she figured out her part in it the better. She wasn't sure why she had taken the job. But something compelled her to continue to see where it would all lead.

So for now, she'd stick around, work with him, have the occasional dinner. See what might come of it.

She glanced at Megan who was perusing the sketches.

"That's my favorite." She pointed to the bronze statue. "It reminds me of the Italian Villa we stayed at when Mom and Dad were alive."

Clare nodded. "That's an original art deco piece. I like it, too."

"What's this?" Megan fingered the folder with the gold digger theme.

"Nothing." Clare tried to grab it.

Megan snatched it right up. "What are you trying to hide? Let me see."

Clare watched Megan's eyes go from a mischievous twinkle to downright surprised.

"What in the world? Is that a tent in the living room? And this?" She jabbed her finger on the pickaxe. "What the heck is that?"

"Okay. Okay. Give it back." She'd better think fast. "It's a design for a Gold Rush theme party." She smiled hoping to steer the conversation.

"You used to do these all the time. When you used to be fun." Megan smiled, but Clare knew she meant every word.

"Are you sorry I'm not fun anymore?"

"Truthfully? Yes."

"These events were few and far between. I need to focus on real design work if I'm to have any success in the field."

"Don't lie. You're doing it for the money and you know it. When are you going to put that silly idea out of your head and take Dad's money?" Megan placed her hands on Clare's forearms. "I don't care if you're fun again, I care if you're happy."

"I appreciate how you feel. I really do."

Megan sighed and focused on the event design plans.

"Okay. You want the real story on this design?"

Megan raised her eyes to Clare's and nodded.

Clare scrunched up her nose. "I'm kinda thinking about implementing it as a form of revenge on someone."

Megan placed her arm over Clare's shoulders, her brown eyes glittering in merriment. "That's the Clare I remember."

Clare nodded, smiling. "This guy is very straight-laced. He's going to walk in expecting something classy and traditional and instead he's going to get this." She tapped her fingers on the folder.

Megan laughed. "I like it. Where did you get this idea, anyway?"

"I got it from that gold digger comment made by Chris's brother." Clare held her breath, unsure of Megan's reaction.

Megan frowned and gave her a cold stare that clearly said, *seriously?*

"The guests will dress in period costume." Clare felt it best to ignore Megan's disgruntled expression. "The women will dress up like saloon girls. Red floozy dresses and everything. Cool, huh?"

"Yeah." Megan's voice trailed off as she went into some zoned-out place.

"You okay?"

"Yeah." She kept staring at the drawing.

"I'm sorry about the gold digger thing," Clare said. "I shouldn't have made light of it."

"No. Really, it's fine."

Megan's frowning expression had gone from foggy and glassy-eyed to a resolute and determined gleam.

"What are you thinking?" Clare wasn't sure she wanted to know, but the transformation on Megan's face compelled her to ask.

"Nothing." Megan brightened and flashed a sunny smile. *Too* sunny.

Clare knew that look. Had been called to the principal's office on more than one occasion because of that very look.

"Now Megan. Don't do anything crazy."

"Who me?" Megan grinned and tucked her arm though Clare's, giving it a good shake. "Thanks for always being here."

Megan's gaze was locked on hers, all glowing and earnest, her eyes the brightest blue. Clare squeezed her hand. "Where else would I be?"

Megan tilted her head. "I can think of a hundred places."

Clare glanced down, nodding at the drawing. "This is what I love, and I can do it from anywhere. So why not here with you?"

"You know what I mean." Megan un-looped her arm from Clare's and strolled toward the door. "I think I'll go back to school after lunch."

"Sure. Okay." Megan *was* up to something. And, maybe that was a good thing. She needed to get her mind on something other than Chris. But, it was probably too much to hope that Megan's faraway look from earlier had nothing to do with the younger Carrington.

Chapter Seven

Will ran the paintbrush underneath the fifty-foot sloop, wiped his brow, and stood at Wes's approach.

"I thought you were on your way to Costa Rica."

"Well, hello to you, too, bro."

Will laughed. "I'm too hot for niceties."

"I don't leave until tomorrow. The remnants of tropical storm Charlene needs to clear out first."

"Good, then you can grab a brush and help me finish up."

Wes picked up a four-inch paintbrush and dipped it in the clear varnish. "You've done a beautiful job on the *Pilot*."

Will nodded and stepped back from the hull. "I think so. In another month, she'll be sea worthy."

"It'll be nice to see her out of dry dock."

"I know. She's been hovering over land far too long."

"She's a real beauty. Fifty feet of pure heaven."

"Where have I heard that before?"

"James, remember?"

"James?"

"Yeah. Pendelikon. It's what his daughter used to say. The one that raced with him."

"That's right." He nodded. "I remember now."

"I never understood why no one in the family claimed the *Pilot*," Wes said.

"Probably because I wired the money the very morning James agreed to sell it to me. Told him it would be in his account by the time he and his wife got back."

Wes slid his hand along the hull. "I would have thought the daughter who sailed would have wanted her."

Will shook his head. "Maybe too much sadness attached."

Wes shrugged. "Guess so."

They worked side by side in silence. Will had wanted to talk with Wes about his handling of Chris and his girlfriend. Now was as good a time as any.

"Listen, I know you and I both want the best for Chris and Cal, but I need you to let me handle this thing with Chris and this Megan girl."

"His gold digger?" Wes chuckled.

"You don't know that."

"That's all any woman is ever after. You and I both *know that*. Better for Chris to find out now before he gets screwed by some skirt."

"Not every girl is Donna, Wes. You can't go around painting all of them with the same brush." He glanced at the one in his hand. "No pun intended."

Wes shook his head and continued to spread varnish over the hull in smooth strokes.

Will sighed. "One of these days, you're going to meet someone wonderful. But if you keep up this antagonistic behavior toward the opposite sex, you're going to miss her."

Wes paused in his strokes and looked him square in the eye. "Don't tell me. You've met someone, right? That's what this conversation is really about."

Will blew out a breath and set his brush on the edge of the varnish can. "I *have* met someone, but this conversation is not about her or me. It's about you being judgmental and accusatory toward women and putting similar ideas into Chris's head. He needs to learn from his own mistakes. Hell, you and I both know he won't have the same experience as us."

"I'm just trying to save him from the pain, brother."

"And steer him where? Into a pitiful existence built on sarcasm and distrust?"

Wes stopped and looked him full in the face. "Yeah, at least he'll be safe there."

They stared at each other for a brief moment, then Wes continued varnishing the wood.

"I understand how you hurt."

Wes burst out laughing. "Seriously, you think this is about what Donna and Phillip did? That I'm somehow emotionally marred for life?"

"The thought had crossed my mind."

"Is it so wrong to want to protect my sensitive side?" He grinned as if to make light of it. As if joking would cover the pain of what had happened.

"Protect away, bro. If that's what keeps you happy."

"It does. So. Tell me about this girl of yours. What's her name?"

"Ha, not a chance." Will dunked his brush into the can of turpentine. "And she's not *my girl*. We're not even dating. I've hired her to decorate the penthouse." He wiped the bristles on an old piece of T-shirt. "There's something about her, though. She's a real enigma."

"Ah, mysterious. That's the best kind. From the looks of you, I'd say the chase is on." Wes slapped Will on his shoulder.

"Except, I think it may be the other way around."

Wes's eyes widened. "You're kidding."

"Just forget it."

"Like hell I will."

Will replaced the lid on the varnish while Wes immersed the brush in the can of mineral spirits to soak. "I really like this woman. She's a knock out. Absolutely gorgeous. But I can tell she doesn't like me."

"Then she's crazy."

"I can't put my finger on it." Will shrugged. "But something's wrong."

"Well, in my experience, when a woman doesn't like a man it's because said man has done something unforgiveable. Which of course, doesn't sound a thing like you. Now *me* on the other hand..."

Will laughed and shook his head.

"What's her name?"

"Sullivan."

Wes cocked his head to the side. "Nope. I can't take credit for that one. It must be men in general she doesn't like."

"I certainly hope not."

"Why don't you just ask her?" Wes said.

"You mean lay my cards on the table, like you?"

"Yes. I keep telling you. Straight and to the point. Works every time."

"Not in this case. It isn't that simple, plus it feels too weird." Will tapped the varnish lid with a hammer, then tossed the hammer in the toolbox. He ran his hand across the back of his neck. "I don't know. I'm playing it out. The penthouse will take some time. So who knows?"

Wes slapped him on his shoulder. "Need any help—"

"No." Will pulled out the brush, slung out the excess turpentine, then rolled the brush in old newspaper.

Wes lifted the varnish can and followed Will to the storage shed. "Let's get cleaned up. Alphonse is steaming crabs."

Chapter Eight

The breeze fluttered across Clare's face like a familiar friend. She hadn't sailed since her parents' accident. Not out of fear, but from sheer self-punishment. Why should she sail when her parents could not? As a teenager, she'd found it hard to forgive herself, thus meting out what she thought the appropriate punishment for her failures, her stupidity, and her parents' demise.

Even though she'd tried not to go out on the water with Will, his persistence had won in the end. So here she was, reveling in the experience. Loving it. Welcoming it back into her life as an old friend.

The breeze lifted her hair from her temples. She inhaled the sea air and thought of the man mere feet from her. Will Carrington annoyed *and* fascinated her. He was too darned good looking, for one. Hard to ignore his dark, wavy hair and dreamy eyes. She'd believed him to be egotistical and arrogant. Except for that first meeting, he was anything but. It was when he wasn't aware of her presence that he became an A-1 jerk.

This Jekyll and Hyde act intrigued her. He was different when they were together. Pleasant. Nice even, but gave as good as he got. She had to admit, she liked that about him. And enjoyed their occasional bantering.

"You're a natural," Will said, interrupting her thoughts.

"I've missed it." She smiled, but it wasn't for him. Her joy in the moment would not let her do otherwise.

"So why did you give it up?"

She focused on her hands as she trimmed the jib for speed. "Time. Money." She shrugged. "You know."

"I know what you mean. Sometimes there's not enough hours in the day."

"The coast is beautiful along here," she said.

"You should see it at night. The Miami lights are magical."

She *had* seen it. Many times, with her stepdad. She pictured his wavy, salt and pepper hair, his magnanimous smile and bronzed skin, reverently holding his image until it was lost in the sea spray. "My dad and I used to sail along here. Day or night, it didn't matter. We had an old sloop. A gorgeous fifty-footer." She licked her lips and swallowed. "But, we lost her in a...storm."

"Oh, no. Was anyone hurt?"

She nodded.

"I'm so sorry."

"Before we got her, we had a thirty-foot sloop. *That* was fun sailing. My dad would keep the tiller and mainsheet in his driving hand and I'd trim the jib. We were a great team and sailed as often as his job allowed."

"As an airplane mechanic he probably had most weekends."

"What? Oh...yes. That's usually when we went out."

"Take the wheel while I make us some coffee."

Will slid from his chair and waited for her to take hold. "I'll just be a minute," he said, then disappeared to the lower deck.

* * *

The aroma of coffee assailed Will's senses. He loved the nutty, bold essence and couldn't recall a time in his life that he didn't. As a child he'd stand next to his father at the counter in the factory waiting expectantly for the moment when his dad placed the freshly ground bag of coffee beans underneath his nose. He'd inhale first, then his father, then they'd both smile.

As this particular Carrington blend brewed, he grabbed two mugs from the upper cabinet and waited. He could tell by Clare's handling of the boat, she was a seasoned sailor. The accident she spoke of must have been terrible for her to give up something she obviously loved.

Three minutes later, he mounted the steps from the galley, a steaming cup in each hand.

He caught his breath. Clare stood, one hand on the wheel, while the other one attempted to tame the unruly brunette strands that whipped around her face. His heart stopped. God she was beautiful. When she noticed him, her lips parted in a radiant smile. Not even Florida's sunniest day could compete with it.

"Here you go." He handed her the hot brew. "Cap's Peaberry. It was my grandfather's favorite bean and after he died my father named this blend in Cap's honor." Good grief. He sounded like a damn TV commercial. He willed his heart to slow down.

"Your grandfather's name was Cap?" Clare took a sip, eyeing him from the rim of the cup.

"It was Jason. He was known as the captain, but everyone called him Cap."

"Did he start the plantation?"

"The plantation belonged to my grandmother's family. She was an only child and my granddad had gone to work on the plantation one summer. They fell in love and eventually married."

"And your grandmother? Is she still living?"

"Very much so. She lives in our family home in the Keys. Here..." He pulled out his wallet. "That's her on her eightieth birthday."

Clare looked into the face of a smiling, silver-haired lady who didn't look a day over seventy. "Wow, she looks great. It's hard to believe she's eighty."

"I know. And still a go-getter." He snapped his wallet together and slipped it back in his jeans pocket.

"So how did your family end up here?"

"My grandfather was from Florida and moved his family here when my father was five. The family has gone back and forth ever since."

"Have you been back lately?"

"No, but now that you mention it, I'm due for a visit."

"Once we get the design finalized, let me know when you're going to be gone for a couple of weeks and I'll get most of the work done while you're away."

"That works for me."

* * *

They docked at the marina and made their way to the car.

"Are you in a hurry to get home?" Will said.

"Not at all."

"I'd like to show you something."

Fifteen minutes later, Will pulled into the driveway of his beach house.

Clare opened the car door and got out. "How charming."

"Thanks. I like it."

"You live here?"

"Surprised?"

"Frankly, yes. I confess, I'd pictured you in something bigger."

"So do my brothers. Hence, the Miami penthouse."

"So, you're a pleaser at heart."

He slid his key into the lock, cocked his head to one side, and eyed her. "Maybe I am." He winked.

After he unlocked the side entrance, Clare followed him inside and stood quietly as he turned on the lights. The entire place was white. From the wood siding that covered the walls to the comfortable linen furniture.

"It's obvious you don't have kids or pets." She chuckled.

Will gave her an engaging, heart-stopping smile. "Come this way."

He led her through the small living space onto the front porch.

"Oh, my."

"Nice, huh?"

"*Very.*" She leaned against the white painted railing and soaked up the view. The Gulf waters spanned in front of them for miles, its waves beckoned as it broke against the shoreline. "Why would you ever want to leave this for the penthouse? You've got the sand at your feet and the ocean just yards away."

"Who says I'm giving it up?"

"I just assumed..."

"*That*, Miss Sullivan, is your trouble."

"Excuse me?"

He took her hand and led her to the end of the porch, then faced her. "You assume way too much." He gently pulled her into his arms. "About me, anyway."

Heart thudding, she gazed up at him. "What are you doing?"

"What do you think?"

In business, Clare had one hard and fast rule—never get involved with a client. As tempting as he was, she made a half-hearted attempt to pull away.

"No. Wait. Don't think." He gently tapped her chin. Her eyes locked with his mesmerizing ones. Blue, like the ocean. Dancing with the light of the late afternoon sun. For a brief moment they roamed over her face, hungry, desiring, then he lowered his head.

His warm lips covered hers, tentative, at first. Questioning, teasing, exploring. Creating a yearning in her soul for more. The scent of his aftershave tingled her flesh with a mixture of sea air and musk.

Unable to resist, she wrapped her arms around his waist just as his arms banded about hers. Something joyful skipped over her heart singing a melody of warmth and affection she'd never experienced with a man. In that moment she wanted more and, just as she was about to ask, he released her.

"Let's take a walk on the beach," he said.

Speechless, she nodded. After they kicked off their shoes, he laced his fingers through hers and led her down the steps. The sand, still warm from the afternoon sun, caressed her feet as she strolled alongside him. Will led her to the water's edge, stopped, and encircled her waist.

"Will, I don't date my clients."

"Shh, just lean against me and watch the sun set," he whispered in her ear. "You don't want to miss it."

Her mind yelled, 'Stop!' but her body obeyed, and she leaned back against his broad chest.

In less than a minute, the sun melted like butter into the ocean. When it was gone, orange and yellow ribbons spread across the prettiest blue sky. Will's arms held her close. Wonderfully warm and secure she rested against him, knowing it would have to end soon enough. Was it so wrong to enjoy a simple moment in time? To grab hold of it when and where you could? Most of her peers didn't think so. But, she wasn't most people. She was an orphan and a mother to a younger sister.

She sighed and relaxed into his broad frame. She'd held the world on her shoulders for so long, she hadn't realized how wonderful it was to lean on someone else for a change. Someone strong, good-looking, and attentive. She'd so enjoyed the afternoon, simply being on the water, sailing. Mostly, she'd enjoyed him. A sudden longing overwhelmed her. A yearning to belong to this man. A heady thought for someone who hadn't even been looking for love. For the first time in her life, she felt complete in Will Carrington's arms. Like finding the lost piece to a puzzle.

Could this be happening? Was it even real? Or was Will Carrington a fake and a phony? A playboy at heart, simply toying with her emotions until he got what most men wanted. And if he did? Then what? She thought about the way he'd spoken about Megan. How could this sexy, sweet man be the same person?

Closing her eyes, she focused her attention on the crashing of the waves. Just one moment longer.

She pulled from his embrace and turned toward him. He gazed down at her with a smile in his eyes. Not with the face of one who could so cruelly dismiss the young heart of a college girl.

He crossed his arms and gave her a friendly once over. "I can see you're going to be a challenge, Clare Sullivan. I should tell you..." Eyes twinkling, he tilted his head. "I'd like nothing more."

She swallowed and blinked, not quite sure what to make of that statement. He was so darn sexy. This man, the one right here and now, this man she desperately wanted to know. Personally, intimately, and forever. But, in light of what she knew about him, was that even possible?

"If that's what you like," she shrugged, "then that's what you should expect."

He raised a brow. "Throwing down the gauntlet so quickly? I like you already." He tugged on a lock of her hair. "How about some dinner. I make a mean plate of shrimp linguini." Then taking hold of her hand, Will led her back to his cottage by the sea.

* * *

So Clare Sullivan was not as cool and collected as she liked to make out. Within seconds of Will taking her in his arms, she was putty, malleable and so damned kissable. When she tightened her arms around him, he was a goner.

She didn't know it, but she'd killed him right then and there. He wondered how far he could have gotten if he hadn't been the one to pull away. The memory of her desire-filled eyes and her trembling 'kiss me again' lips would have to hold him for a while.

There was still a mystery to be solved. Extraordinary kiss or not, Clare emphatically did not like him. Even when she was acting all pleasant and malleable, he could tell she was holding back.

His experience had proven more times than he could count, that 'trust and women' didn't go together. He and Wes were the same in that regard. But that was no way to keep living.

It didn't mean he didn't enjoy the occasional flirtation.

If nothing else, Clare Sullivan ignited the desire to explore his options. He'd been drawn to her from that first moment in the restaurant.

In his former years, he'd always been the one to trust first, only to find disappointment at the end of the rainbow. Then, out of the blue, steps a woman who mistrusted him. And from that instant he had to know why.

But, he'd been honest about one thing. He did like a challenge. And he'd given her fair warning.

She was opening one of the cabinets, pulling out plates as if nothing had happened. Poised and in control. How'd she do that, when his heart was still racing from that moment on the beach?

While she set the table, he grabbed the spaghetti from the cupboard, then set the shrimp out to thaw.

"You seem comfortable in the kitchen," she said.

After running cool tap water over the shrimp, he placed them in the sauté pan. "I live alone, so it comes with the territory, I guess."

"Before I sing your praises, I'll have to give this dish a taste test first."

Her smile rendered him a one-two punch in the gut. Steady ol' boy. He pulled his eyes from her merry ones and focused on the linguini sauce.

Twenty minutes later, they sat at the table overlooking the dark ocean.

"If this tastes as divine as it smells... But, no pressure."

He groaned. "Yeah, right."

For a few minutes they ate in companionable silence. Clare lifted a napkin to her lips. "I'm impressed. In more ways than one."

Will lifted his wine glass to his lips, took a sip, then sat back. "Well, that's a relief." He grinned.

"Seriously." She threw her hand over the darkening view. "You could buy this entire stretch of beach and yet you live simply, cook your own meals, and delight in the daily sunset."

"Is that so shocking?"

"Not shocking, but the penthouse seems...oh, I don't know, much too opulent for the way you choose to live."

He smiled. "I'm a man of many interests. Take you for instance."

"Me?"

"Yes, you. We've been working together for a few weeks now. I've answered your questions, spent time with you, and yet I know very little about you."

She dropped her gaze and pressed her lips together. The subtle move was not lost on him. He watched, fascinated with her sudden interest in her wine glass. Her refusal to look him in the eye intrigued him. She continued to toy with the stem, a sure sign she was either uncomfortable or hiding something.

For someone who wore the mantle of poise and self-control so well, she sure didn't know how to play the game of love and attraction. In this moment, she seemed more like a teenage girl on her first date, than a successful business woman. Odd for a woman with her looks and talent. Surely, that couldn't be right.

Nope. She was definitely hiding something. Her entire countenance signaled, 'Stop, don't get personal.' Was it simply a matter of trouble opening up to others? Or, something deeper?

"So, tell me. Who is Clare Sullivan?"

Her lips parted in a hint of a smile. "You're right, I've been the one asking the questions. But, let me remind you, that's part of my job. If I'm supposed to design your home, the place you come to each night after working all day, the place where you'll eventually bring your bride and have your family. If I'm to do all of that, I *must* ask questions."

"And you still haven't answered mine. Who. Is. Clare. Sullivan?"

Her expressive features held a brief note of concern, then it was gone.

"Come now, I'm not asking you to tell *all* your secrets."

Her eyes flew to his. *Well, that certainly hit a nerve.*

"Just one or two." He smiled.

She raised her chin and looked right at him. "I was orphaned at sixteen and had to raise my little sister."

Any humorous comeback he'd planned died on his lips.

"So you said earlier. And I'm sorry. I had no idea you were so young when that happened and that a younger sister was involved."

"It's okay, but I'd rather not talk about it."

"Then why did you bring it up? Surely there are other, less painful things you could have shared with me."

She gazed at him for the longest time, then shook her head. "I don't know why."

He wondered if her parents' death was related to the disappearance of the fifty-foot sloop? It would make sense. Anyone who loved sailing as much as she did would only give it up because of a tragedy.

He reached across the table and took hold of her hands. "Maybe you wanted to tell me. Maybe, you *needed* to tell me. Is it so hard to open up to me? Am I some ogre to be feared? I like you, Clare. A lot. I enjoyed kissing you. A lot." He smiled. "I'm interested in taking our relationship to the next level."

Clare's lips parted. "Which is?"

"Do I really have to spell it out for you?"

"Yes."

He sucked in a deep breath and blew it out. "All right. I think about you all the time. I can't wait until we meet, even if it's just to talk about fabric options." He squeezed her hands. "I simply want to get to know you and if anything comes from that, then great. What do you say?"

He gazed deeply into her eyes. Eyes that questioned and searched his face as if she would find some sort of answer there. Eyes that battled over her decision. He'd surprised her. Could she really be that naive not to read the signs he'd given her for the past few weeks? He wanted to smooth the crease in her forehead. To feather kisses along her rigid jaw until she moaned for his lips to cover hers.

"So what do you say?"

A dimple appeared at the side of her mouth. "I enjoyed kissing you, too."

He stood, pulling her to her feet. She stepped into his open arms and he held her close. *Now we're getting somewhere.*

* * *

Clare floated through the front door into the sprawling living area of the Pendelikon penthouse, still tingling from an amazing day in Will Carrington's company. She tossed her Gucci bag on the ornate side chair tucked against the wall just inside the door.

When she'd pulled into the garage, she noticed Megan's car, so she went in search for her. She found her sister slouched on the sofa watching TV.

She was in the midst of texting and as soon as Megan noticed her, she quickly swiped at a tear.

"Hey, are you okay?"

"Hi. Yeah." Megan shifted and tossed her phone on the seat next to her. "It's nothing."

Clare nodded. She knew when to push Megan for information and when not to. She sat back against the cushions and looked at the TV screen. It was the old romantic comedy, *Pillow Talk*. "I remember this movie. Doris Day finds out Rock Hudson's the womanizer who shares her party line and the same man who's been duping her for weeks."

"I know. It's really cute. I love it when she agrees to decorate his apartment, but unknown to him she's planning to turn it into a gaudy, brothel-like man cave."

They sat in silence and watched the large flat screen. Megan's phone buzzed. Clare's eyes drifted to the thing, then back at the TV.

"Idiot. Stupid. Jerk," Megan said.

"What?"

"Chris. It's over between us. Thanks to his control-freak brother." Megan lifted angry, tear-filled eyes, and stared at the TV.

"Honey, maybe it's for the best."

Open mouthed, Megan spun toward her.

"Or, I could talk to him."

"Sheesh, Clare. I'm not ten years old."

"Then *you* talk to him. Tell him who you are. If you really care for Chris, at least tell him the truth. Then he can deal with his brother. As a matter of fact—"

"But I'll look like a fool. Besides, it still doesn't negate what his brother said about me."

"No, but I'm sure he's a reasonable man." She thought about today's events with Will and knew this to be true. She'd tell him herself, but knew it would be embarrassing for Megan. "Will you at least think about it?"

"Fine." Megan jumped up and ran from the room.

Clare huffed and stood to her feet. "Thank you, Will Carrington."

Clare needed advice. The only person she could trust was her dear Edward. Minutes later, she was standing in front of Edward's private quarters. She could hear the drones of his TV coming from the room. She tapped on his door and waited.

"Miss Clare. Come in."

"Hey, Edward. Got a minute?"

"For you. Always."

Clare smiled and stepped through the doorway.

"Please, sit down."

"Thanks." She let out a heartfelt breath and followed him to his TV room, then sat next to him on the sofa.

"What are you watching?"

"Football. It's a home match at Wembley Stadium. Nothing special. It's early in the season." He lowered the volume.

She leaned her head against the back cushion and watched it with him. "Don't you miss it? Going to the games yourself?"

"Sometimes, but I haven't played since the mid-seventies."

She turned her head to look at his profile. "Dad told me you were an amazing athlete."

"So the papers used to say."

"I'm sorry your football dreams didn't come true."

"Some of them did. I have no regrets."

She nodded.

"What is it, Miss Clare? Something's on your mind to bring you to this part of the house."

"I know. I haven't been to see you in a while. I'm sorry."

"So what's on your mind?"

"I'm working with this client, and he seems to be two different people. He acts one way with me, but seems to act differently with others."

Edward gave her his full attention. "Are you concerned about him?"

"Not really. I'm just trying to figure him out. I've heard some things about him that are out of character for the person I've come to know."

"Sounds like the *Strange Case of Dr. Jekyll and Mr. Hyde.*"

She laughed. "It does, actually."

A familiar twinkle entered his eyes. One he always held especially for her. He leaned forward and opened the English pine box where he kept his playing cards, then held them up. "Care for a rematch?"

"Of course." She nodded as he began to shuffle the deck. "Edward, forget what I said about you getting a life. Don't you dare leave us."

CHAPTER NINE

Can I talk to you?" Chris walked into Will's office with a face filled with concern.

"Sure." Will rose from his desk chair. "What are you doing home from school?"

"It seems you and Wes were right. After spring break, Megan changed into a completely different person."

"Not who you thought she was?"

"Nothing like."

He put his hand on Chris's shoulder. "Sorry, buddy. I know you like her. Come. Sit." They each took a chair by the windows.

"I mean..." Chris sat forward, agitated and restless. "I thought she was different. But this honest, adorable, *I like you for you* line was just an act."

"Mmm, so the real *her* came out, huh?"

"I'll say."

Will nodded. "That can be quite a shock."

Chris shook his head. "I thought I had her figured out."

"That was your first mistake." He propped his feet on the coffee table. "Figuring out a woman takes years of experience and even then..." He shrugged. "It's still a challenge."

"I guess Wes was right all along." Chris sighed. "But how could he know?" He slouched deep into the chair and shoved his hands into his pockets.

"Experience, for one."

"I can't imagine anyone pulling anything over on Wes."

"Trust me," Will said. "It's been done."

"Tell me."

"Sorry. That's Wes's story to tell."

It was an ugly story and one Will would rather not think about. On the night before Wes was to be married, he'd caught his fiancée with one of his best friends. Only twenty-five at the time, Wes had been devastated by the experience. After that, his trust in women plummeted to a big. Fat. Zero.

Will understood Chris's disappointment. Hell, he'd experienced it more than once himself. But, it didn't make seeing Chris suffer any easier. When it came to the opposite sex, both he and Chris had to learn the hard way. It was in their DNA. *Suckers.* That's what Wes and Cal had called them on more than one occasion.

At least *he'd* displayed some evidence of caution where an attractive woman was concerned.

A pair of luminous, emerald green eyes infused his thoughts.

He'd done his best not to let a woman get *too* close.

Pink full lips clouded his vision.

Who was he kidding? He balked whenever one prodded him with too many questions. That's why he'd teased Clare at the Miami coffee shop about her third degree. Even though it had been her job to ask questions, he'd refused to let his guard down with her. Self-preservation and instinct had kicked in, and he'd resorted to mockery. Which had proven in the past to keep the opposite sex at a safe distance. Emotionally that is.

Physically was a different story. It didn't mean he didn't enjoy the occasional flirtation. He was a man after all. And at thirty-five, he now knew how to play the game. He'd certainly enjoyed his share of female company. A woman in his arms was a delight.

But to have the *right* woman in his arms had been sheer heaven.

Yet, something was going on with Clare. He just couldn't quite put his finger on it. One thing was certain though, she did make him want to take a chance again.

Chris was texting, a frown on his face. He looked up and flushed.

"Is it Megan?"

"Yeah. She wants to know if we can meet."

"Really?"

"Yeah, really."

"So what are you going to do?"

"I don't know." He shrugged. "Maybe play her game for a while. See what comes of it."

"Where have I heard that before?" he mumbled.

"What?"

"Nothing. Just be careful, little brother. Sounds like this Megan could chew you up and spit you out."

"Don't worry." Chris stood and headed for the door. "I've got her number. If you know what I mean."

He certainly did. Chris was learning. For a split second he was saddened by that reality. He thought about the couples he knew that were happy. At least it seemed so on the surface. Who really knew?

Chris's phone buzzed. "It's Wes. We're getting together for lunch before he heads out. Wanna come?"

"I've got a meeting in thirty minutes. Unless you need my support while he gives you his 'I told you so' speech."

Chris laughed. "I think I can handle it. Besides, I might get his advice on how to handle Megan."

Will sat back down to prepare for his meeting. He could only imagine what Wes would have to say. He bet, plenty.

* * *

Clare flipped open her file to the Carrington project, while the waitress at Larry's Lunch Box topped off her coffee. She'd chosen an earthy, warm color scheme, which was classic in design yet both functional and comfortable. Except for a few definite masculine pieces, it was very close to what she would choose for herself. Surrounded daily by the vibrant tropical colors of south Florida, it was a nice change to go with the more subtle, less intrusive charcoals, tans, and creams.

As she perused the design, she made notes in the margin. Sipping her coffee, she glanced up. Will was such an enigma. Nothing about the man she'd come to know was anything like the man Megan spoke of. He was warm and funny and sexy as heck.

She'd found herself more and more attracted to him as the days and weeks went by. There had to be an explanation for his odd behavior. She was anxious for their upcoming meeting. Tired of the secrets, it was time to come clean, and she hoped he'd be receptive. She'd more than enjoyed their time together and had searched for any excuse to see him before the appointed time. She clamped her teeth over her lower lip and smiled.

I've got a crush on you, Will Carrington.

He'd said he wanted to take their relationship to the next level. Her body tingled at the thought. That's what she wanted, too.

At that moment, Will Carrington pushed through the front door, glanced across the room, then gave the hostess a nod indicating he knew where to go.

Clare sucked in a delighted breath. She lifted her hand, surprised when he didn't notice her. His handsome features held a thoughtful expression as he strode with purpose down the aisle, one over from where she sat. He walked right past her and slid into the booth behind the lattice wall that separated them. The tightly woven web-like pattern made it difficult to clearly see who was on the other side, but not enough to hide their conversation.

She wondered if she should say something. She certainly didn't want to get caught looking like she'd been eavesdropping. But Will's next words completely negated that idea.

"So I was right about Megan," he said.

"Man were you ever." The younger man sighed.

Clearly this was Chris. Clare squinted between the spaces of the lattice for a closer look. Like his older brother, he, too, was dark-haired and from what she could see, quite the looker.

"I hate to say I told you so."

"But you just had to say it anyway, didn't you," Chris said.

"Is it my fault you don't listen?" Will shrugged his wide shoulders. "I keep telling you—trust your older brother."

Will's deep voice scorched her ears. The saying that one never heard anything good about one's self while eavesdropping was certainly true. Hard not to with them sitting right next to her.

Lord, why hadn't she had the sense to move to another table? A knot formed in the pit of her stomach. She should have alerted Will that she was here. What if he discovered her?

"I know, I know." Chris forked something on his plate. "Boy did she have me fooled."

Clare froze. Too late to let them know she was here. Maybe if she got up slowly, she could slip out without being noticed.

"Wrapped you around her little finger, did she?"

"I'll say."

"What was your first clue?"

"She started dressing like, oh I don't know...over the top. Low cut dresses, tons of makeup. Not like her at all."

"Popped open her top button, did she? As soon as they expose a little cleavage, they know it's over for you."

Clare gripped the edge of the table until her knuckles turned white.

Will lifted a French fry and pointed it at Chris. "This girl knows exactly how to ring your bell. It's what they all do." Will slid the fry between his lips. "Bat their long lashes. Form their full lips into a seductive smile, then *bam!* Try to take you for everything you're worth."

"Enough already," Chris said. "I feel beat up as it is."

"Trust me. I've had my share of encounters with the likes of her. Gold diggers want only one thing."

"And that is?"

"Status. They walk around with a sense of entitlement, using their boyfriends as stepping-stones to a more fabulous life. Each one richer than the last."

"I thought she was different. I really did."

"Tell me. When you two go out, who pays?"

"I do."

"Exactly." Will took a bite of his sandwich and for a second they ate in silence. "Sounds like you missed a real doozy, though. That's the good news."

"I guess," Chris said.

"My advice. In the future. Turn and run. As fast as you can."

"Yeah. To the nearest exit," Chris said.

"Do not pass go," Will added.

"And do not collect two hundred dollars."

They both laughed.

"Believe me, knowing her kind, that would be a small price to pay."

Sarcasm oozed from his lips, crushing her as she sat in silence. Even if she'd wanted to speak, she wouldn't be able to.

"Sounds like you know from experience," Chris said.

"Experience is a fair and exacting teacher. Lessons can be learned on both sides."

"What do you mean?"

Will leaned forward. "All I'll say is that I had my ways of making sure the little darlings also learned from the experience."

He sat back, and Clare could just imagine his expression. All smug and self-assured. In that moment, she hated him.

"I should add, tears were involved. So be prepared."

"What kind of lessons?"

"That, little brother, is something you'll have to figure out for yourself. No two women are alike. My advice may not work for your little miss. Although, there was one I let play me along for quite some time. I acted the charming, wonderful lover, and when she thought she had me hooked, I dropped her."

"I want details," Chris said.

Clare squeezed her eyes shut. Her limbs weakened, and she began to shake. Her heart pounded and her stomach churned, shredding her insides like the lettuce on her plate. She'd heard enough. She thought about how hurt Megan had been over Will Carrington's cruel and callous words.

At first, she'd wondered if her sister had exaggerated, as she was sometimes prone to do. But if this cruel, macho nonsense was an example of what Megan had overheard, she could see why her sister had been upset.

Heat infused her limbs, and she trembled with anger. She sucked in huge amounts of air to steady her racing heart. Tears stung her eyes. She glanced at the webbed pattern next to her. Will's deep chuckle reverberated through the trellis and spurred her to action.

"I'll leave the details for you to figure out," he said. "Does she have any family?"

"An older sister."

"Maybe you should introduce me?" He chuckled. "I'm overdue for a challenge."

Her lunch soured in her stomach. She quickly gathered up her designs and stood. She could *not* sit here another second.

Clare bolted from the restaurant and hurried to her car. She angrily swiped at her tears as she pressed the accelerator and sped down Gulf Shore Boulevard. Why, oh why, didn't she say something? How could she have been so blind? It was as if Will Carrington was two, completely different people. How could the well-mannered professional she'd come to know be this arrogant, cocky jerk?

She huffed out a breath. "The two faced—" Clare wanted to swear. But years of holding her tongue came through again. Gritting her teeth to keep herself from doing just that, she yanked the steering wheel left and entered the parking garage. Tires screeched as the Prius skidded to a halt beside the family Bentley. Will's verbal bullets rang over her head, and she ran toward the elevator as if wanting to take cover. As the doors closed, she knew she had to pull herself together before entering the penthouse.

Once inside, she stopped and stood in the middle of the foyer, fully expecting Edward to appear, but he didn't. Good. She needed some time alone.

She entered her office, tossed the Carrington file on her desk, and flopped down in her chair. She placed her elbows on the desk and shoved her fisted hands to her mouth. How could she continue to work with him after this?

She gnawed on her bottom lip, sat back, and flipped open the file board. Fingering the Belgium linen between her fingers, she thought about how beautiful she could've made his penthouse. She'd loved sharing her ideas with him. Foolishly thought they'd developed a kinship, something she'd secretly hoped they might build upon. But he wasn't who she'd thought. She'd been deceived, duped, misled. Maybe if she'd had more experience with men she would have seen it coming.

"What's the use? The last thing I want to give this man are my best ideas." She snapped the file closed. He'd been a compelling figure, physically *and* emotionally. Pulling her in all directions since the day they'd met.

Admit it. You're heartbroken. You liked him. A lot.

She stood and paced. She had no other choice. He'd have to find someone else.

CHAPTER TEN

Clare glanced around her office. She knew trying to work on another job would be a fruitless effort on her part, so she spent the rest of the afternoon going through some files and her messages.

Three hours later, she pushed back from her desk. Even though it was still cluttered with paint chips and carpet samples, she didn't have the emotional energy to clear it for the day.

She picked up Will's file just as muffled voices floated from the foyer. She glanced at her watch. Megan must be home. She wedged the file between several others on the credenza behind her chair.

"There you are." Megan stood in the office doorway, dressed in a snug fitting, low-cut dress. "Come out here. I want you to meet someone."

Clare could hardly keep her eyes off Megan's dress as they moved down the hall toward the living room.

Seated on the sofa, accepting a coke from Edward, was a good-looking dark-haired young man about Megan's age. There was something familiar about him.

"Clare, this is Chris Carrington. Chris. My sister, Clare."

Chris immediately stood and held out his hand to her. Clare caught her breath. He favored his older brother, especially in the hunky looks department. She could understand Megan's attraction to him.

No doubt about it. He was the same young man who'd been with Will at Larry's Lunch Box. The same young man who'd definitely sworn off Megan, less than four hours ago. What was he doing here? What had the two of them discussed after she'd left? Did they have some plan?

"Hi, it's nice to meet you. Thanks for having me this weekend." He gave her the most engaging smile.

This weekend? "Of course." Pretty much stunned by this turn of events, that was about all she could think to say.

Clare hastily glanced at Megan who was looking at her with eyes that pleaded, 'please don't blow this, I'll explain later'.

Clare pressed her lips together to keep from blurting out the obvious question, then eyed her sister with a look that said Megan would have some explaining to do.

"We're so happy to have you. Um, I was just about to make a sandwich. Chris, make yourself comfortable. Megan and I will just be a moment."

She didn't wait for Megan to respond, but grabbed her sister by the arm and pulled her none too gently from the room. Once out of earshot, she swung her around to face her.

"What the heck is he doing here? And why are you dressed like that?"

"This dress is a Lea Sin. All the girls in my sorority are wearing them." She twirled in place. "Cute, huh?"

"You look like...a cocktail waitress."

Will's scathing 'low cut and cleavage' remarks suddenly clanged through her brain.

Clare studied Megan's face. "Are you wearing false eye-lashes?"

Megan grinned. "Chris is here because I invited him." She looped her arm through Clare's. "Since when do you have a problem with me inviting a friend home for the weekend?"

"You know our home has always been open to your friends, so don't try turning this around. You know darn well why he shouldn't be here. Have you forgotten his tyrant of a brother? Knowing him, Chris is probably being tailed. It would be just like him to barge right in here and demand an explanation."

"How would you know what his brother's like?"

"I... He..." Clare threw up her hands. "I just know." She huffed out a huge breath. "Look, there's something I need to tell you—"

"Relax, will you? Chris is not being tailed. Anyway, I don't know why you're all up in arms. I'm the one who's been maligned by the big, bad Mr. Carrington."

Clare yanked open the fridge. *You've got that part right.* She pulled out the ham and cheese, while Megan grabbed the mustard and the oat bread. Clare peeled back the plastic on the ham, then slid the meat from the packet to the cutting board. She slathered mustard on a slice of bread and glanced at her sister. "What are you up to, Megan?"

"Nothing." Megan's lips scrunched into a smirk.

Clare stopped spreading mustard and rested her fists on the counter. "Sweetheart. I may have been born at night, but it wasn't *last* night."

"Seriously, Clare. That is *so* middle school." Megan folded a slice of cheese and stuffed it between her lips.

"Then stop acting like you're still fourteen."

Megan ripped open a bag of Lays, poured ample amounts of the crispy chips on each plate, then lifted the tray.

"I've got this under control. Okay? I'm just having some fun."

"And what about Chris? Is he having fun, too?" Clare said.

"Of course."

"And I suppose that 'get up' you're wearing is part of the fun?"

"Darn right, it is." Megan winked and left the kitchen.

* * *

The weekend was mostly uneventful until Clare walked in on Megan and Chris Saturday night. 'Making out' was way too tame a phrase to describe what they were doing on the sofa.

"Megan!" Clare shrieked her sister's name as if a bus were about to hit her. Two sun-tanned bodies parted like the red sea. Arms and legs untangled in record time, then flailed frantically through the air snatching up previously discarded garments that moments before lay serenely on the carpet.

After a moment of shock, Clare turned away. She gathered her wits as the yanking of fabric and zippers played in the background. She turned back to Megan and Chris as they shot to their feet, both red-faced and unable to look her in the eye.

Clare held her breath. What in heaven's name had gotten into her sweet little sister?

"Chris." Clare heaved a deep controlling breath. "You need to leave."

He glanced at her, then at Megan and nodded. "I'm very sorry. I'll see myself out." He exited the room and didn't look back.

Clare stared at Megan and shook her head. "What were you thinking?"

"It's not what it looked like."

"It looked like you were about to have sex."

"We both still had on underwear."

Crushed, Clare plopped on the chair opposite Megan. "I know you're growing up, honey. I just wasn't prepared to see this in our home. I can't control what you do at school—"

"I don't do this at school. I never act this way. I was only trying to teach the Carringtons a lesson."

"What are you talking about? What kind of lesson?"

"They think I'm a gold digger. A slut. Well then that's what I'll be."

Clare opened her mouth, then clamped it shut. She sat stunned. For the first time in her life, she had to really think about what she needed to say to Megan. Her little sister was not a young amiable kid anymore, but a young woman.

"First of all, a gold digger is not necessarily a slutty person."

Megan raised her blonde brows and eyed Clare with a look that clearly said that was the most idiotic thing she'd ever heard.

"Okay, you're right. That was stupid. But, how in the world will your behavior punish them? You're not a gold digger and until five minutes ago, I would have sworn you weren't a slut either." She shook her finger in Megan's face. "But, make no mistake. Using your body to teach some guy a lesson *is* slutty."

Megan crossed her arms and slouched against the sofa.

"I realize I'm not that much older than you. And I know you've been hurt. But you need to think long and hard before you continue down this path. This is not the way to handle things."

"Look, I admit I got carried away," Megan said. "And, I'm really sorry I offended you, but I know what I'm doing." She stood, marched to the door, then stopped. "You're not going to want to hear this."

"What?"

"I got the idea from you."

"Me?"

"Yes. You."

Clare sat stunned. "How on earth—"

"Your gold rush theme party. The one you're designing."

"Oh. Yeah, well..." The same idea had also crossed her mind, so she couldn't very well scold Megan for trying it, as well. "Still. Promise me this won't go any further."

"I'm in the middle of a plan. And I intend to see it out. Good night."

Clare flicked out the hall lights, then continued down the hallway to her bedroom. "If I get through this, I'm never having kids."

* * *

Clare waited in the outer office at Carrington Enterprises. *Just walk in and get it over with.* She drew in a slow cleansing breath.

"Would you like a cup of coffee while you wait?" Carol said.

"No, thank you." The last thing she wanted was food or drink. She hated confrontations, but this had to be done. Will was a towering and forceful figure, and she'd have her work cut out for her to keep control of the situation.

She'd give Will the updated design, then tell him he'd have to find another decorator to implement it. She was through. She'd decided she wasn't going to tell him the real reason why. His conversation with Chris had left her hurt and humiliated. The last thing she wanted right now was for him to know she'd been eavesdropping.

The door to his office opened. As usual, he was dressed immaculately, his custom-made pin-stripe suit encasing his broad shoulders to perfection.

"Clare." His smile dazzled, lighting up his face from clear across the room. "I didn't know you were coming today." He stepped forward and took her hand in his.

"I wasn't planning to, but something came up, and I wanted to get you the preliminary design plans. At this point, it's just a rough draft."

"Of course. Come in." He led her back to his office and held the door for her to enter. "Is everything okay? You look upset."

She tried to smile, but it fell flat.

"Please, sit down." He motioned to one of the upholstered chairs.

"I can't stay. I just wanted to give you this." She handed him the folder with the preliminary design. *Tell him now. Just spit it out.* "It's basic at this point, and pretty straightforward."

"I'm sure it's fine."

"Another designer will be able to pick up where I left off."

"What do you mean? What's wrong?"

"I'm sorry. A family situation has come up, and I don't think I can finish the project."

Concern etched his features. "Is there anything I can do?"

Yes. Stop being a jerk to my sister.

She shook her head. "No. It's just something I need to take care of."

He took her hands in his and gently squeezed them. An action that clearly evoked a response from her, as he knew it would.

She seethed inwardly and gazed up at him. His brow creased, and his firm lips pressed into a worried frown, presenting the perfect picture of concern. Boy, was he good.

She glanced away. He was faking it. She knew the man in the restaurant was the real Will Carrington. With no audience in attendance except for his younger brother, there was no need for him to perform as he was now.

"I wish you'd reconsider." His smile wreaked havoc on her inner regions. Blast the man. He brushed his hand down the length of his tie. His voice lowered. "I feel like you know me."

She gazed into his eyes. *You're darn right I do.* It took all of her concentration to keep her disdain from coming through.

"The real me," he continued. "And let me tell you, not many do." He chuckled softly, tilting his head in an effort to get her to look at him.

She'd adored that low chuckle of his, but now...

"Is there any way you could stay on? Maybe hire another assistant to help you?"

Will's words at Larry's Lunch Box still stung. *Take you for everything you're worth — acted the charming lover, then dropped her...* Clare shivered. She would not let his cunning behavior work on her.

Just tell him he's a good for nothing jerk and get the heck out.

But she stood there looking at her feet. How could she be *so* weak in light of his attitude toward Megan? His conversation with Chris at Larry's gave her a renewed purpose. He was doing to her what he'd done to all the women who'd gone before.

"Well, maybe if I did have some help." She watched him for his reaction and was almost undone by his earnest and eager, boy-like expression.

So this is what it was like to "hook, line and sink" someone. She rather liked the sensation, especially when she could turn the tables on a low-life such as him.

"Look," he said. "I've loved everything you've shown me so far. If it helps, you don't have to do another thing." He dropped her hands, then ran his fingers through his dark hair. "Heck. Just do anything you want with the place."

She stared at him. *Did he really just say that?* "Anything?"

"Yes." He handed the plans back to her. "Just don't quit."

She quickly stood with the newfound desire to teach him a lesson. By God, someone needed to. How many young women had this man hurt? It had to stop.

"All right. You've convinced me. But, I really do have to go."

She left his office, making her escape before she said something she would later regret. It was all she could do not to run. She closed the door behind her and paused. This was one design plan she would more than enjoy implementing.

Carol was looking at her with an odd expression. Clare smothered a smile and hurried toward the exit. "Bye, Carol."

* * *

What the heck just happened? Will ran his fingers through his short crop of hair. What was he thinking giving Clare carte blanche to do whatever she wanted to his six million dollar penthouse? Wes's words rang through his head. 'Be careful you don't do anything crazy.'

Sure, he'd spent a lot of time with Clare and trusted her professional opinion, but seriously, this *could* be considered crazy. He knew for a fact it *would* be in Wes's book.

And since when did he become some groveling fool? *Since you can't think of anyone or anything else but her.*

Okay. It was one thing to be smitten with a beautiful, talented woman, but entirely another to hand over a million-dollar project to her.

Will ran his hand over his Hermes tie and sat down in one of the side chairs. "Carol!"

She popped her head in the doorway. "Yes, boss?"

"Did anything happen to Clare while she was waiting for me? A phone call or anything?"

"No, but she did seem rather uptight. I offered her coffee and was surprised when she turned it down. The few times she's been here, she's raved about our coffee. Is everything okay?"

"I'm not sure. Something was definitely wrong. She was going to quit. Some family issue. But I talked her out of it, and now I'm not sure why."

"What do you mean?"

"Well." He started to laugh. "I think I've just been hoodwinked."

"Hoodwinked?"

"Yeah, you know, duped. Taken in. Conned."

Carol shook her head and smiled. "I know what it means. I just haven't heard it since my grandmother was alive." She leaned against the doorframe. "Are you saying she's deceived you in some way?"

He got up and stepped over to his desk. "I have no idea, but I have every intention of finding out."

"Hmmm, maybe you need to talk with Wes." Her eyes twinkled.

"Don't even joke about that, just get Ken Barton on the phone for me."

Carol laughed and pulled the door closed behind her.

Moments later, she buzzed through. "Ken's on line two."

"Thanks."

Will swiveled his chair to face the window. "Ken. How's it going?"

"I can't complain. What's up?"

"Did you know I hired your friend, Clare Sullivan?"

"No, I didn't. How's she working out?"

"Great, actually. She's extremely talented."

"So what's up, buddy?"

Will could tell from his tone that Ken was smiling. He was a longtime friend from his college days at Florida

State. And at times, much easier to talk to than any of his brothers. "Well, she's not an open book if you get my meaning."

Ken laughed. "Keeps her cards close to her chest, does she?"

"Something like that."

"From what I hear, you're not the first who'd like to break her shell."

So she has a shell? "What was she like when you worked with her?"

"We were on a couple of projects together, but now that you mention it, I can't say I know much about her personal life. On the job, she's known for her impeccable taste and beautiful designs."

"So, you know nothing about her past? Her parents? If she has siblings? Anything?"

"Her parents died years ago, and I believe she has a younger sister, but other than that I'm clueless I'm afraid. Sorry I couldn't be more help. If I think of anything else, I'll let you know."

"Sure, thanks."

Will sat back and steepled his fingers underneath his chin. Something had obviously rattled her, if the sudden lack of color in her face was any sign. "What are you up to, Clare? And why did you make it so easy for me to convince you to stay?"

Chapter Eleven

Clare brushed her teeth, slipped on her nightgown, then curled up in bed with her laptop and the gold digger file. As she flipped through her notes, she thought about her earlier conversation with Will. *Anything, he says, huh?* That certainly worked for her.

Clare was never one to hold a grudge, but this project was going to be one for the books. She'd fallen to temptation, but not the 'under his spell' kind. This was payback. Time to teach Carrington a lesson and Clare Girl would do it.

As she read, the idea of just how to decorate Will's condo took shape.

"Since he's enamored with gold diggers, it's only fair that he enter their world. Therefore, I'll surround him with the latest, most innovative and readily available tools and equipment of the gold digging trade. Including his very own, personal gold digger. Me."

* * *

Clare entered Will's office after hours, wearing a sexy, tight-fitting outfit she was certain he'd find difficult to ignore. When she entered, his ready smile faded as his gaze traveled from her Christian Louboutin pumps to the gold medallion dangling between the hollow of her breasts.

"Are you...going somewhere after this?"

"No." Clare smiled and proceeded to spread out the design plans on his conference table.

Will stood next to her, perusing the layout. His tanned, clean-shaven face knit into a frown.

"Well, what do you think?"

He eyed her with a mixture of awe and disbelief.

"Not me." She pointed to the table. "My proposal."

"Forgive me if I have trouble focusing. You look incredible."

Her low-cut blouse offered a view he obviously had trouble ignoring.

He licked his lips and focused on the plans. "I like it. But I'm not crazy about the gold figurine. It seems a bit..." His gaze inched back to her spiked heels and snug outfit. "Gaudy and flamboyant."

She locked eyes with his, and she wondered if there wasn't another message in his words. Oh, she certainly hoped so.

"Well." She shrugged. "If you think so. I can see how it might be off-putting to you. How about I keep digging and show you some different options in a day or so?"

He took hold of her hand and noticed her bracelet. "That's quite a set of rocks."

She flicked her hand in the air. "Just a bobble I wear on special occasions." *Like when I'm trying to teach some idiot man a lesson.*

Her parents had given it to her on her sixteenth birthday, to mark her special day. *Emeralds, for their green-eyed girl.*

"It's beautiful."

"Thank you."

"Tell you what." He looked her up and down. "Since you're dressed for a night out, why don't we go to Mereday's for dinner, and you make the decision about the figurine."

Bingo. That certainly worked for her. She smiled and nodded. "Fine. Just leave the details to me. And I'll do my very best to design the space to reflect the person that you *truly* are."

The real you.

"I promise, you can trust me to do that."

"I have to admit, it feels strange giving up control in something of this magnitude without at least some input."

She stacked the design drawings together. "I know you're concerned about giving me carte blanche, but it's done all the time."

He ran his hands down her bare arms. "Well, maybe when you're done with the penthouse, we can take another trip. A longer one this time. Say to St. Johns."

Mister, after I'm done with you, the last thing you'll want is to take a trip with me. Long or otherwise.

* * *

Shortly after they were seated at Mereday's, a stocky waiter went over the evening's specials, then took their cocktail orders.

After the waiter left, Will leaned in, placed his elbows on the table, and gazed into Clare's eyes.

"I didn't think you drank," he said.

"Tonight, I'm making an exception." She gave him a glittering smile, then glanced around the restaurant. "I love this place. Expensive *and* delicious."

"It is that." He eyed her with uncertainty. "And I must say, you look quite the dish yourself."

The waiter returned with their drinks. "Any questions about the menu?"

"No. I think we're ready to order. Clare?"

"Yes, I'll have the roasted stuffed quail with the ciabatta stuffing and steamed asparagus."

"Very good. You, sir?"

"I'll have the Creole shrimp with Nueske's bacon and the cheddar grits."

"One of my favorites."

"And bring a large bottle of S.Pellegrino for the table," Will said.

"Oh, and this bottle of wine." Clare pointed her red-nailed finger to a name she couldn't even pronounce, but the price was sooo right. Four-hundred and ninety-eight dollars. *Right.*

"Excellent choice, miss."

Will's eyes widened, and he turned completely white. "Clare—"

She gave him a beguiling look, reached across the table, and took hold of his hand. "You don't mind, do you? I feel like tonight is a celebration of sorts."

After a brief hesitation, he nodded to the waiter, who tilted his head, then left.

Clare lifted her diamond-clad hand to the candlelight. "Look. It's casting tiny rainbows on the ceiling."

He stared at her like she was from another planet. "So, what are we celebrating?"

She gazed at him and deliberately fluttered her lashes. "Simply being alive." Then giving him her most dazzling smile, she dropped her gaze to finger the emerald bracelet at her wrist.

Will blew out a disgusted breath.

Delicious. Her evil plan was working.

"Was it a gift?" He practically huffed the question out like the big, bad, wolf.

"Bryan Gifford gave it to me. We broke up shortly afterward. He told me to keep it." She shrugged. "But, I'd planned to anyway."

"I thought women returned expensive gifts after a break up? It must have sentimental value?"

"Sentiment has nothing to do with it." She deliberately raised a brow. She'd practiced in the mirror and hoped she'd pulled it off. "The guy's loaded." She gave the bracelet a flick of her wrist, then reached for her raspberry martini, pulled out the olive, and slid it between her lips. "Mmmm, what is it about a plump olive soaked in vodka?"

He blinked and stared. He ran his hand up his Hermes tie, stopping at the knot at his collar. He swallowed, lowered his hand to his drink, then lifted it to his lips. She suspected he needed a drink right now. She watched as he raked his eyes over her upper body. She'd chosen this low cut, tight fitting dress, hoping to display her *assets* to her advantage.

* * *

Will swallowed, then eyed her from across the rim of his glass. Clare sat back, perfectly relaxed, and gazed around the room. A slight smile played along her red lips, an all-knowing twinkle peeking from underneath her long lashes.

Stunning.

Beguiling.

A vamp of the first order. He blinked and stared. When did she start wearing false eyelashes?

Clare Sullivan had tied him into knots.

Worse, she knew it.

Her actions were deliberate and calculated. So, she wasn't the stylish, no nonsense, business professional he'd first thought. She'd confused the hell out of him with this new and unexpected side of her. Who was the real Clare? The elegant, well-dressed, designer, or the sexy, gold digging vamp, who even now disregarded his very presence.

He clenched his jaw. She seemed more interested in the man at the next table, whose gleaming-eyed response angered the hell out of him. Not that Will could blame him. What man wouldn't respond to such an enticing package?

As the evening progressed, he noticed Clare wouldn't look at him and when she did, it was only a quick glance. As if she couldn't trust herself to hold his gaze. As if it would reveal something she didn't want exposed. If that were the case, then this was indeed a game. He needed time to think. It was probably a good thing he was leaving soon.

He signaled the waiter for the check.

"Clare."

She took a deep breath, causing her chest to rise, then turned to face him. Was there a particular reluctance in her eyes? Hard to tell with that single, sassy, cocked brow of hers.

"Are you sure you want to implement your design on the condo? Because I get the feeling—"

"Oh, absolutely. I've thought of nothing else for days."

"I could postpone my trip to Costa Rica."

"No. Take your trip and don't worry about a thing."

"All right." Though he agreed, it was against his better judgment. "If you have any questions, Carol knows where to reach me."

Chapter Twelve

The following week, Will left for Costa Rica, and the timing couldn't have been any better for Clare. The two weeks he'd be gone would give her plenty of time to outfit his condo with the gold digger theme. Between Internet orders and scouring antique, salvage, and junk stores for the rest, she'd already acquired a healthy stash to work with.

She gazed at the sparkling array of gold and jewels safely locked under the glass counter at Myra's Antiques.

What was it about gold that mesmerized?

What kind of woman used men just to acquire such finery? Easy for her to say, since she could buy the contents of the entire case. But even if she couldn't afford it, she'd never date or go after a man only for what she could get from of the relationship. Rich or poor, she'd want a man only because she loved him, and he her.

Since her parents' death, she'd never had time for love. Maybe if she'd been dating someone when the accident happened, things would have been different.

As she roamed amongst the aisles to see if anything was appropriate for her gold rush theme, her gaze fell upon a full length, ornate, gold-framed mirror. The gold flecks in the glass gave it a saloon honky-tonk feel that she loved. The perfect replica for Carrington's design surprise.

A few minutes later, she spotted a flamboyant brass balance scale with weighing dishes on each side. Too good to be true. Even though she'd already bought two rustic antique scales for the condo, she couldn't let this one go. Nothing rustic about this one. It screamed western saloon brothel.

She fleetingly wondered why a brothel would need a measuring scale. The brass naked lady spread her arms wide as if to receive her lover and from each hand hung matching brass weighing saucers. She was blindfolded like Lady Justice, but there was absolutely nothing *lady-like* about her. Clare caught her lower lip between her teeth as a giddy sensation crept up her shoulders and neck.

"Perfect."

"Will that be all?" Myra asked.

"For now. Put both the mirror and Miss Risqué Lady Justice on my account."

"Seriously?" Myra's wide-eyed, questioning stare brought a smile to Clare's lips.

"Yes, seriously."

"Well, either you've developed a taste for 'god awful,' or you have a client with really bad taste."

Clare chuckled. "If it's so tacky, then why is it in your store?"

"A friend dropped it by." Myra rolled her eyes. "She's going out of business so I'm trying to help. But trust me, that was the only thing I could take." She shook her head. "You should see the rest of her stuff. Nothing but junk I'm afraid."

"Where's your friend's place?"

"Over on Charlotte. It's called The Tick Tack." Myra grinned. "But it's Tick Tacky if you ask me."

After Clare put them on her account, she hit two more junk and antique stores that afternoon without much success. Her hopes in finding something acceptable at The Tick Tack ended in disappointment as well. There wasn't much left to buy except for a set of well-used, tin dinner plates and cups. Perfect for a campsite meal display.

At this rate, it would take forever to find what she needed. So that evening she pulled up the sites she'd bookmarked on the Internet. She methodically placed her orders and with each click, her smile grew. Too bad no one was actually going to go to this lavish event. It was by far the best theme party she'd ever planned.

When money's no option, it's amazing what one can do.

Will had given her an extra key so she could enter at her leisure. She inserted the brass key and seconds later the elevator doors opened to the marble-floored foyer of the penthouse.

She paused to enjoy the beautiful carved crown molding depicting the art deco era. Too bad she intended to desecrate it with what she had in mind.

Her gaze followed the arched doorways. Even in their original finish, they still invited one to wander off to wherever they led. Of course, she wouldn't touch the perfect structural elements standing before her, but neither would she enhance them.

"Forgive me," she whispered.

Just one final walk through with the plans, and tomorrow her team would begin.

* * *

Clare and her assistant, Brenda, stood side by side, then high-fived each other in pure satisfaction.

"It all looks fantastic," Brenda said. "The brassy effect of the gold adds a particular gaudy decadence."

Clare chuckled. "It does, doesn't it?"

"This is where you shine, Clare. Three years ago, I attended one of your theme events and when you stopped doing them, I have to confess, I was disappointed. I'm glad you're planning them again."

"Don't get your hopes up. This is probably just a one-time thing."

"Either way, this is going to be *some* party."

Clare had led Brenda to believe the design was for a special event. And it was. A 'putting a man in his place' event.

"And the gold," Brenda gushed. "Oh, my gosh. I thought it was way too much at first, but I love how it shocks when you first enter. And it only gets better as you stroll through the condo. I swear you're a genius. Mr. Carrington and his guests will love it."

"Thank you, Brenda."

"Has Mr. Carrington seen it yet?"

"Oh, no. And not a word if you talk to him. You and Carol can't say a thing. I'm meeting him here Sunday night. I want it to be a surprise."

* * *

Saturday afternoon, Clare was on her way home from putting the final touches on Will's apartment when her cell phone rang. She checked the caller ID. It was Carol.

"Hey Clare. Will's back in Naples sooner than expected. He said something about going to Miami. I wanted to let you know since the penthouse is supposed to be a surprise. And if I know my boss, he won't wait until Sunday night to see the place."

"Oh, right. Thanks for giving me the heads up. I'll do my best to stall him."

Clare punched Will's number in her phone and waited. No answer. *Dang.*

She made a U-turn at the next intersection and headed to Will's cottage. After stopping to pick up a dinner-for-two basket from Shade's Kitchen, she arrived at his place in record time.

She grabbed the basket, then scurried from the car. *Please be here.*

Seconds later, she rapped her knuckles on the side door. She glanced at her chest and quickly undid a couple of buttons, then planted a smile on her face.

A few moments later, Will opened the door. Shirtless, barefoot, and wearing only jeans.

Caught off guard by his muscular torso, Clare just stood there staring. Dark stubble covered his jaw, displaying a rugged five o'clock shadow that was sexy as hell.

* * *

Will took pleasure in watching Clare's glorious smile fade. Her radiant eyes briefly widened, and her lips parted in surprise. She licked her lips.

"Hey you." She gazed expectantly up at him.

He lounged against the doorframe, giving her a nice view of his bare chest.

Two can play this game, sweetheart.

He wondered which Clare had come to visit, and had the distinct feeling she was trying to gauge his reaction to her sudden appearance.

"Carol called and told me you came back early." Her words came out in a rush. "I thought I was supposed to pick you up at the airport tomorrow, then we were going to drive to Miami to see the penthouse together. But—"

"Take a breath," he said. "You were. But my plans changed." He held the door open. "Come on in. I was just getting dressed. Let me grab my shirt."

She followed him inside, and he could feel her eyes on him. He lifted the polo shirt off the back of a chair, pushed one arm through, then the other before slipping it over his head. He turned toward her as he adjusted the fabric over his torso.

"Did I come at a bad time? You weren't going out were you?" She gazed up at him with all the innocence of a little girl.

"Now that you're here, I wouldn't dream of going out. What's in the basket?"

"Dinner. I hope you haven't already eaten." She strolled past him into the kitchen and got out a couple of plates. "It's such a lovely night, let's eat on the porch."

He followed her outside, sat down on the wicker loveseat, and watched her flit around like a butterfly, from flower to flower.

She opened the basket and proceeded to set out the picnic spread of fried chicken and potato salad. When she was through, she spun toward him. "I hope you're hungry. I just love Shade's fried chicken baskets."

"Me, too." He spread his arms across the back of the loveseat. "I had one last night." This time he deliberately gave her his best innocent expression.

"You... When did you get home?"

"Yesterday afternoon."

He took no small delight in deceiving her, but her expression in that moment was about his undoing. Her merry eyes darkened in anxiety, and her pretty mouth dropped open.

"Is that a problem?"

She shrugged and glanced at her hands. "Of course not." She smiled, engagingly. "It's just, if I'd known, I'd have come yesterday. So. I guess you don't want chicken."

"Come here." He laced his fingers around her arm. In one lithe move he had her across his chest and secured snugly against his body. She licked her lips, fluttering her lashes in uncertainty.

He gazed into her wide, questioning eyes and kissed her. She stiffened, and he raised his head.

"Something wrong?"

She shook her head and ran her tongue along the side of her mouth. "Just a bit unexpected." She fluttered a smile. "You seem different. Not quite yourself."

"Kind of like you the last time we were together."

Was that her heart beating like thunder against his chest? He raised his hand and lightly smacked her bottom.

"Hey!" Something between confusion and humor crossed her features. "What's that about?" She laughed uncertainly.

He brushed his lips along her cheek and jaw line. "Something about you brings out the primal instinct in me." His lips hovered over hers. "I thought you of all people would like it."

"What's that supposed to mean?" Her breathless voice caught in her throat.

"Anything you want, darlin'." Her heart continued to race through the thin fabric of her dress. Enthralled at the myriad of emotions that tumbled across her face, he banded his arms around her.

"Look, if you're suddenly into *Fifty Shades* you can count me out. But I suspect I'm finally seeing the *real* you." She squirmed and placed her hands against his chest.

"Going somewhere?" Amusement tinged his voice.

"Let me go," she said through clenched teeth, pushing firmly against him. Right as she did so, he loosened his hold, and she tumbled to the floor, her floral print dress sliding up to her thighs.

"Uh, oh." He sat up and offered her a hand. "Are you okay?"

She grabbed both sides of her skirt and tugged them over her knees. Refusing the offer of his hand, she scurried to her feet, brushing her hair from her flushed face. "Actually, I am. But I get the impression you really couldn't care either way."

"On the contrary." He stood and stuffed his hands into his pockets. "I care tremendously."

She stomped over to the table and grabbed her purse.

"Leaving so soon?"

Her chest heaved. "I've suddenly lost my appetite." She spun on her heel and headed for the side door.

"Are we still on for tomorrow night? I can't wait to see what you've done."

She skidded to a halt, then without looking back, gave a stilted nod.

"Good. I'll meet you there," he yelled at her departing back. "Say around seven?"

She nodded again, then climbed into her car.

He leaned against the doorjamb and watched her drive away.

And if you fail to show up, I'll come and get you.

Back inside, he entered the kitchen, then crossed the tile floor that led to the porch. Fried chicken assailed his senses. He grabbed a chicken leg and bit down. He hadn't had Shade's fried goodness in months.

He made himself comfortable while he chewed the crispy, perfectly seasoned meat. But at the moment it tasted more like cardboard. Tomorrow night's showdown couldn't come soon enough.

CHAPTER THIRTEEN

On Sunday, Clare wrestled most of the day with whether or not she would show up at Will's penthouse. The drive alone was a deterrent. After all, it wasn't like she hadn't seen the place. And it was obvious from last night's performance that he'd already set eyes on it.

She pressed her fingers to her temples. Wasn't this what she'd wanted? A showdown with Will Carrington? A face-to-face moment of truth?

Frankly, she wasn't inclined to return to the scene of the crime. She'd lost all element of surprise. Now that he knew, what was the point? His reaction to it, to her...

Oh, God.

Mortified, she placed her head in her hands. Best to face the situation and him.

Two hours later, dressed in her 'power outfit', navy jacket and skirt, she squared her shoulders and with a forced confidence, entered the elevator to his penthouse.

She'd stewed and argued and practiced what she wanted to say all the way from Naples to Miami. Butterflies fluttered deep in her mid-section. She sucked in a deep breath, then held it to the count of five.

The elevator doors opened just as she exhaled. She took one step then stopped.

At least twenty-five people were mingling in the outer foyer of the condominium. A sudden drop in Clare's blood pressure darkened the small space. *No!* She leapt back, landing against the wall, and grasped the brass handrail.

"There you are." Will strode with purpose, threw one hand up to block the door from closing, and took her by her arm.

Clare dug her heels into the carpet, and he had to practically drag her forward.

"Come. Don't be shy. We've all been waiting for you." He gave her no choice and ushered her into the middle of his friends and colleagues. "This is Clare Sullivan, my designer. I've given her carte blanche and, like all of you, I'm anxious to see what she's done with this vintage 1920's Miami penthouse jewel." He looked pointedly at her, hammering each word like nails in a coffin.

"May we have a drum roll, please?" A guest spoke from the crowd and everyone laughed.

Clare's stomach churned. Now would be a good time for the world to end.

She grabbed his arm, clutching his jacket with all of her strength. "Will," she whispered with desperate urgency. "Why are all these people here? When you know what I've done—"

"I'm christening the place with a party. My board of directors are in town and I was planning to have a dinner for them anyway. So I thought, why not here? A sort of house warming." His eyes glistened down at her. "I'm sure what you've done will delight us all."

This *could not* be happening. "But—"

He patted her arm and spoke so the group could hear. "I'm sure it's fine. No one will notice if a few things aren't finished yet."

"This is *not* what I'd planned." She hissed through clenched teeth. "You've had your fun. Make all these people go away right now."

Her words fell on deaf ears as Will placed his hand on the brass knob. She clutched his shirtsleeve, but was too late. He pushed the door open.

A hushed silence fell over the group as everyone filed in. Wide-eyed, mouths gaping, they slowly turned to take in the gold and gaudy décor in all of its hideous glory.

She wanted to die.

Will's stony profile revealed little of what he must surely be thinking. But after yesterday's confrontation, she could only imagine. Clare raised a hand to her throbbing temple.

"What a sight," one man said. "It's outrageous."

"What's this?" a female voice chimed from the front.

"Oh, look," said another.

Clare stole a glance at the woman. The expression on her face was one of delight. And that smell. Clare took a deep breath. Roast beef and hot bread assailed her senses.

She stood, stunned. A gorgeous woman dressed in red taffeta paused in front of her. Bright yellow feathers spiked from the cluster of dark curls piled high on her head.

"Would you like a beef biscuit?" she asked.

Clare shook her head and watched the saloon girl approach another guest. A pop came from across the room as a waiter, dressed as a cowboy, opened a bottle of champagne.

In a dazed-like trance, Clare moved from the foyer to the living room and watched the merriment of a party. A honky-tonk ditty chimed from the player piano she'd had delivered just days before.

She swallowed. Will stood a few yards away with an older couple. He must have felt her gaze, for he turned at that moment and stared at her. His eyes mocked as he raised his glass in her direction, more to impress those around him than to salute her. His cold, but brief, glance cut to the core.

A floozy server in bright blue paused and offered her the crab claw appetizer. Clare shook her head and stepped back. She couldn't stay, but she wanted to talk to Will before she left. Needed to tell him why. That was the whole reason she'd implemented the design. To be able to tell him off. Shake her finger in his face.

She'd rehearsed what she wanted to say more times than she could count, and now that she had the chance to do so, she recoiled from the idea. This was not the venue she'd planned. A showdown was now inevitable, but she had no intention of having it here.

As she turned to make her escape, an attractive woman in her fifties approached her.

"Hi, I'm Ellen Forbes, and I absolutely adore what you've done here. I've used scores of designers, and I've never been as impressed with them as I am with you. Yours is a rare talent." She beamed. "Here's my card. I'd love to talk with you about an event I'm planning in my home in Boca Raton."

Shocked at such a reception, Clare pulled herself together. "Um, of course." She retrieved a business card from her purse and handed it to the woman.

"Thanks. I'll be in touch," Ellen said.

Clare edged past a merry group who were taking turns weighing the fake bags of gold on one of three Lady Justice scales she'd placed throughout the penthouse.

Once in the foyer, she gazed at her reflection in the tall gold-flecked mirror. Shame engulfed her. She'd never meant anyone but him to see the place. Yet somehow he'd known. And like any savvy businessman, he'd turned his humiliation into opportunity.

"I see the ashen look has been replaced by a subtle pink hue. A few weeks ago I would have seen that as an adorable trait. Today, it screams guilty conscience."

She turned slowly at the edge in his voice.

"I really don't know why I don't—" He ran his hand through his hair. "I've treated you with nothing but respect."

"Except for my sister."

"Nice try. But since you're the only Sullivan I know, I find that accusation unlikely."

"You hurt her. Said things about her that weren't true."

"If she's anything like you, I'm sure it was well deserved. But don't change the subject. I don't have a clue who your sister is and right now, I don't care. Right now it's about you and me." He jabbed his finger in her face. "Just thank God I managed to pull your spiteful scheme off for my grandmother's sake."

"How did you know?"

"I got back earlier than I'd expected and had already planned to have the board party here. It was going to be a surprise. *For you.*"

"What do you mean?" Her heart thudded madly in her chest.

"I wanted to introduce you to my peers. To show off what was *supposed* to be your beautiful work."

"Oh."

"I had to get something from my desk and was greeted with this...*spectacle*. After the initial shock, it only took a few phone calls to change the food and the servers outfits to fit the ah...crime."

At that moment, a petite, but elegant older woman approached them.

"Clare," Will said. "I don't believe you've had the pleasure of meeting my grandmother, Mary Carrington."

Warmth flooded Clare's cheeks, and she forced a smile.

"Grandma, this is Clare Sullivan, my designer."

"Oh, my dear." Mary clasped Clare's right hand and squeezed. "I absolutely adore what you've done here. Will has told me how talented you are, and I can now see what he was talking about. You must redo my little cottage on Carrington Key." She turned to her grandson. "And no arguments from you, either. The cottage is what I need at my age. I'm tired of rambling through that big house when I visit."

Clare glanced hastily at Will. "Well. I... Thank you. I'd love to, but I'm not sure, I mean..." she stammered.

"What Clare is trying to say is that I'm not quite through with *her* yet."

His double meaning wasn't lost on her.

"But once I am, she'll be all yours."

"That's fine, then." She beamed from one to the other, completely oblivious to the tension between them.

Mary leaned toward Clare and gave a conspiratorial wink. "I keep hoping one of my grandsons will get married and fill that big old rambling house with some great grandchildren for me."

Clare forced a smile. A second longer, and Will's shrewd grandmother would know something was up. As if he could read her thoughts, Will motioned to Carol and nodded toward his grandmother. Carol understood immediately and had Mary mingling with another couple moments later.

"Just so you know, I never meant for anyone to see this but you," Clare said. "This whole thing was a mistake."

"A mistake? I saw the plans. My name was across the top. Of Every. Blasted. Page. Look at this place. Lanterns for lighting. Dynamite crates for tables. Posters of scantily dressed saloon girls all over the walls. Gold mining supplies in the corners of every room. This is what I paid for? Are you kidding me?"

Clare swallowed. "Actually—"

"And that." He jabbed his finger in the air. "What the hell is that?"

She followed the line of his index finger to the object across the room.

"A sluice box."

He downed the rest of his champagne. "You know. I don't even care anymore. You can see yourself out."

He turned away, his long strides separating them in seconds.

* * *

"Will. I had no idea you were so extravagant." Meredith Garner, the wife of his CFO, sparkled up at him. "Where have you been hiding it all these years? And who designed this for you? Quick. Give me her name." Meredith chuckled.

Before he could respond, his assistant hailed her from across the room.

"Oops, gotta run," Meredith said. "But I want your designer's name and number." She flitted away to meet Carol.

"Will. This party is brilliant." Bill Freeman, a board member of Carrington Coffee, slapped him on the back. "How did you come up with the idea? It's the most fun I've had in years."

Another compliment. If his friends only knew. "I can't take the credit. It was my designer's brain child."

"This is more like a *Wes*, than a *Will* Carrington party. I'm surprised, really." Bill chuckled and shook his head. "Seems you're more like Wes than we thought."

"Who thought?"

"The board. Oh, don't tell me I've hurt your sensibilities." He smiled and laid his hefty hand on Will's shoulder. "You're both known for your great taste and hospitality.

Yours is usually a bit less flamboyant, that's all. But this," Bill nodded across the room, "is incredible."

"Thank you. I think."

Bill threw his head back and laughed. "If you don't want compliments, then don't outshine your brother."

"I'll keep that in mind."

"Where is he, by the way?" Bill said.

"Costa Rica."

"You mean he hasn't seen this place?"

Will shook his head.

"His loss."

"I'm glad you're enjoying the party. Why don't you grab a plate and I'll join you shortly. I need to make a quick phone call." Will didn't like to lie, but his head was spinning, and he needed a moment to himself.

"Sure, don't let me keep you. Take as long as you need."

Will slipped into his study and closed the door. *Seriously?* Did the entire board think he was incapable of a good time? They'd rained down compliments for this gaudy, sensational mess since they'd arrived. This was not his doing, but he didn't have the nerve to tell them any differently.

He scanned the room. Clare had even decked this space out in 1849 gold rush paraphernalia. He spied a humidor on the rustic sideboard piece spanning the wall nearest him and opened the lid.

He wasn't much of a smoker, but did occasionally enjoy a good cigar. He picked one from the box and looked around for something to snip off the end. To the right of the box sat a double-blade cutter. It seemed Clare had thought of everything. He cut off the end and proceeded to light it. A few puffs later he was eyeing the tip in enjoyment.

Had he been too hard on her? Deceit and deception were the Achilles Heel of any relationship. But as he took in the canvas pup tent, the panning supplies, and the little bags of fake gold, he couldn't help but smile.

He picked up one of the tiny cotton bags and held it in his palm as if trying to gauge its weight. Then tossed it in the air a few times for good measure. Balancing the cigar and the cotton bag in one hand, he untied the yellow thread with his other. He set the cigar in the ashtray, then shook out a small amount of the golden bubble gum in his hand. It brought back his childhood when his mom would buy the small bags for him and Wes. He slapped the sweet gold nugget gum bits into his mouth, then grimaced. Cigar mouth and sugar did *not* mix well.

He spit out the gum, then retrieved his cigar. Along one of the walls, Clare had framed black and white photos of gold mining camps. Rugged men in work clothes swinging picks against rock, and some on their knees panning in streams. There was a framed certificate from Gold Prospectors Association of America. He blinked. His name was on the certificate. He scoffed out a half laugh-half expletive. "Unbelievable."

Stacks of *The Pick & Shovel Gazette* covered the top of a low-sitting, rustic table centered in the room. Clare certainly had a flair for details.

He sauntered over to the credenza. He picked up *Gold Mania in The Yukon* and flipped through it. His gaze fell on a paragraph and he read, "The 49ers borrowed money, mortgaged their property, or spent their life's savings in pursuit of the kind of wealth they'd only dreamed of. They left their families, their businesses, and their way of life to make that arduous journey."

He thought about his own wealth. Handed to him and his brothers as caretakers. Not one of them had made the kind of sacrifices this article spoke of. As for his great grandfather, that was another story.

He tapped ash from the cigar, then lifted it to his lips.

What drove a man to give up everything, even stability, to go after something seemingly unattainable? Was it the hope that it would be possible? To make a better life for those he loved? That would be a risk he'd never take. There were more sensible ways to making a living, to better the lives of those you loved.

And Clare? What had driven her to act out this charade? Revenge for some sister he didn't even know? It was ridiculous.

He took another draw on his cigar and thought about his own motivation and drive over the past few weeks. He blew out the smoke.

Truthfully, he'd been in a rut of sorts. Especially as far as relationships with women were concerned. And the mystery surrounding Clare Sullivan had captivated him. If he was honest with himself, she'd been the gold he'd sought. The gold he thought he'd found, only to discover he'd been fooled.

Fool's gold. Brass-yellow pyrite with its glittering metallic luster that could fool the best of them with its superficial resemblance to the real thing. He'd been the fool all right. That was the painful truth.

He was just like the 49ers who'd been deceived, even heartbroken upon discovering that the shiny substance they'd found had little value compared to the gold they'd dreamed of.

For a moment, he gazed at the tip of his cigar. Clenching his teeth, he stubbed the lit end against the glass tray, then tossed it in the trash.

* * *

"The party was a huge success." Will's grandmother settled herself on the gilded settee in the living room. "Your designer is an absolute darling."

"You think so?"

"I do. Where did you find her?"

"I met her at a restaurant in Naples. She came highly recommended."

"Well, she's very talented." She sighed and glanced around the gold-rush-themed room. "I wonder how she found all of this? I hope you paid her well."

"She charged plenty. But don't worry, I plan on giving her a huge tip in the near future."

"That's good." She patted his hand. "Do you like her?"

"I did."

"I thought so."

He eyed her suspiciously. "What are you getting at, Grandma?"

"I could tell something was off between you two. Did you have a tiff?"

He gazed at his grandmother in wonder. "Your astuteness knows no bounds."

She playfully smacked his arm. "Don't mock me."

Her aged, but shiny countenance told him she didn't miss a thing. He gently laid his arm over her fragile shoulders. "Okay, truthfully? I was hoping this girl was the real deal." He shrugged. "But now, I'm not so sure."

She squeezed his hand. "I like her. She has honest, caring eyes."

"When she looks at you, maybe."

His grandma chuckled.

"She seems like a special person. Why, look what she's done here. The detail and extravagance amazes me. I'm telling you she put a great deal of thought into your party. This didn't happen overnight. It's obvious she's been planning it for some time."

He chewed the inside of his lip and studied the room. "I'll say."

He thought about this sister of Clare's. At the time he'd been too angry to continue the conversation. Now he wished he hadn't been so rash.

If the accusation in Clare's eyes was to be trusted, then something unpleasant had happened, and she believed he'd been responsible.

"You know what I think?"

Will kissed her cheek. "What?"

"I think she likes you."

"You do, huh?"

"I do."

"I don't know." He shrugged. "But you're right about one thing. This design certainly took some forethought and planning on Miss Sullivan's part."

"Now you're talking." She patted his knee. "Now go make up."

CHAPTER FOURTEEN

Monday morning, Clare awoke from a restless night and sleepily drifted into the living room. She curled up in the corner of the sofa and hugged a pillow to her chest.

She'd certainly made a mess of things. And she didn't even get to tell him off. That was the real disappointment.

Liar.

She closed her eyes against her nagging, insightful conscience. She didn't want to listen to it right now. She wanted to sit and simmer and yell at Will Carrington. But Clare Sullivan never made a scene. Never raised her voice.

Still clutching the pillow, she rested her head against the arm of the sofa and groaned. She had absolutely no idea what to do next. Should she apologize and send him the legit finalized plans for his condo?

Wait.

She sat up. Nothing had actually changed. Last night, she'd just had an audience. She could still follow through.

She'd always planned to have the gold rush décor removed after he saw it, so she'd handle that first.

Then she'd figure out a time and a place to confront him. Tell him what she'd heard at Lenny's and reveal who he and his younger brother had maligned. In her opinion, he'd gotten off easy.

Somewhat renewed with her plan of action, she went into the kitchen for a cup of coffee.

After breakfast, she got dressed and walked down the hall to her office to call Carol. She needed to let her know Theo would be picking up the upholstered furniture and that she'd schedule the movers for the rest. At that moment her cell rang.

"Clare."

"Laney, how are you?"

"I wanted to tell you how much I love the yellow and white stripe and to thank you for putting up with me," Laney said. "I know I can be demanding at times."

"The yellow *does* look better. I'm so glad you like it."

Brenda entered her office and laid a note on her desk. Clare mouthed, "thank you," as Brenda left.

"You were absolutely right, Laney. But most importantly, you're happy. And when you're happy, I'm happy." Clare hung up, stood, then stretched. Laney was a royal pain most of the time, but Trust Fund or no Trust Fund, her expensive tastes helped to pay Clare's bills.

The note Brenda left was from Ellen Forbes, the woman she'd met at Will's gold rush party. Seemed she was at her Boca Raton estate this week and wanted to talk about planning a theme party for the fall. Clare gave her a quick call.

"Thank you, Ellen. I'd love to help you out."

"Wonderful. We're having a few of our friends for the weekend and would love for you to join us. We'll have plenty of time to discuss everything, and who knows, you might even get a few more clients out of it."

"That sounds great. I'll look forward to it."

After they hung up, Clare dialed the number for Carrington Coffee.

As the phone rang, Clare held her breath, hoping Will had not let Carol know the truth of the situation.

Carol answered after the second ring.

"Hi, Clare. Mr. Carrington said you might be calling."

"He did?"

"He told me to let you know he had everything removed except the upholstered pieces. Oh, and he said he'd stay out of your way so as not to inconvenience you."

His way of saying he won't be there. She guessed she should be grateful for small favors.

"He said for you to use your key, then leave it in the condo when you're finished."

"Sounds good. I'll have my upholsterer pick up the rest."

"Great. And may I say, that party was one of the most creative I've ever attended. It was fantastic. And it was totally because of your theme. I actually learned a thing or two about panning for gold, too. Such fun."

Two days later, she and Theo met at Will's apartment.

"Theo, I know it's a bit of a drive from Naples, but thanks for coming on such short notice."

"No problem. Did everyone enjoy the party?"

"Oh, yeah," she nodded. *Everyone except the host.*

As promised, Will was nowhere to be found. But her heart still skipped a beat as she turned the key to enter. She slowly opened the door in case he was standing there with one of the pickaxes.

Relieved to see the place was empty, she waved Theo and his assistant inside to retrieve the sofas and side chairs. There were seven pieces in all, and they were in and out in less than two hours.

After Theo left, Clare took one last walk through. All the glitter and garish décor were gone. The place was again empty and waiting for the love it deserved. Sadly, she knew she'd not be the one to see it through. Her actions had forfeited that pleasure.

She hung her head. The entire point was to put *him* in his place. Instead he'd put *her* in hers.

All that work for nothing.

She sighed.

And she still hadn't figured out how and when to confront him. She wasn't even sure if she'd have the opportunity now. Of course, she could barge into his office, but Carol would be there, and she didn't relish anyone else hearing what she had to say to him.

* * *

"Feeling sorry for yourself?"

Clare spun around. Wide-eyed, caught off guard, and wearing only white shorts, sneakers, and a green T-shirt, she was beautiful. With her lips parted in surprise, he had the sudden urge to take her in his arms and kiss her until she cried *uncle.*

She'd pulled her hair into a ponytail revealing her slender neck. It was the first time Will had ever seen her without makeup. Her brow glistened with sweat. All vulnerable and pink-cheeked from working, she looked like an adorable teenager.

She stood uncertainly and brushed a wayward strand of hair from her face. "I thought you weren't going to be here," she said.

"I lied."

She opened her mouth, then clamped her lips together.

Good. He'd finally shut her up, but unfortunately, it only lasted a second.

She raised her chin. "Well, now that you're here..." Her eyes sparked, ready for battle. "There's something I intend to say."

"Really? An accusatory tone coming from you? That's rich."

She licked her lips, and he waited for her to continue. But it seemed she'd had a change of heart, because she moved to go past him.

He stepped in front of her. "Not so fast."

She stopped, just short of his chest, and took a step back.

"Don't worry," he said. "I'm not here to hurt you. Although, I must admit that for the past couple of days, I've fantasized about a few methods of torture I'd like to apply in your instance."

She sucked in a sharp breath, bristling like an offended porcupine. "I see the real Will Carrington finally emerges," she bit out.

He ignored her remark. "As much as I'd like nothing better than to follow through on those fantasies, this visit is about my grandmother."

Clare's sparkling eyes filled with suspicion.

"She wants you to decorate her cottage." He held up a hand. "No. Let me rephrase that. She *insists*."

Clare crossed her arms as disbelief spread across her features. "I'm sure you'll have something to say about that."

"Not as much as you might think."

"I find that hard to believe." She sidestepped, and he grabbed her arm, stopping her in mid-stride. "Mary Carrington may seem like a sweet, compliant elderly woman to you, but believe me she's ruled the Carrington men with her dainty, iron fists for as long as I can remember. And I for one have no intention of going against her."

"Speaking of iron fists." She eyed his hand, which still clutched her arm.

He released her. "So, what do you say? Help an old lady out?"

She huffed out a breath. "Okay. But, it'll have to be next week. I'll be out of town this weekend meeting a client."

"I'm gone this weekend, as well. So next week is fine."

"Why do I get the feeling you're up to something that has absolutely nothing to do with Granny?"

He shrugged. "You'll just have to wait and see."

For a moment, he thought he'd lost the battle of wills, but as his grandmother had always told him, 'you have to fight for the woman of your dreams, for she's worth her weight in gold.'

"All right. I'll do it. But only if you're not involved."

He shook his head. "Out of the question, since I'll be paying for it."

"Awww, afraid to give me carte blanche?"

"Do you blame me? Now. Was there something you wanted to tell me?"

"I did, but it can wait." She handed him the brass key and walked out.

Chapter Fifteen

What is she doing here?

Will clearly hadn't expected Clare to be one of Ellen's houseguests. She stood across the room, mingling with several people out on the lanai. Her radiant smile rendered a one-two punch to his gut. He fleetingly wondered if she would suffer the same reaction when she saw him.

"Will." Ellen approached. "There you are. Set your bag in the corner. It's a beautiful night, so most of us are already on the patio." She dashed liquid gold into a tumbler and handed it to him. "I believe you know most everyone here. Except for Senator Ralph Bingham. He's our state senator from New York. Recently divorced and on the hunt for wife number three."

They ambled across the living room.

"I see my decorator is here."

"Yes. Mitch and I are going to use her for a big blowout this October. We're thinking zombies."

"Whatever floats your boat, Ellen."

They made their way across the room toward the open doors.

"I thought after your big bash you'd be impressed," Ellen said. "Don't tell me you've lost your fun streak already?"

He rolled his eyes making her laugh as they stepped into the night air. Clare was standing with her back to him.

Will shook hands with the senator. "Nice to meet you," he said.

Clare stiffened and turned slowly toward him. Mouth gaping, her wide eyes went from disbelief to distrust. She didn't say one word. Didn't have to. Her white knuckled, death grip on her wine glass said it all. So much so, he feared it might shatter. Then she visibly relaxed and turned away.

He could imagine what was running through her beautiful head and wondered between the two of them, who'd be the first to come up with an excuse to leave?

As the others turned to talk with someone else, he approached her from behind.

"So this was your weekend plan," he whispered in her ear.

"Did you know I'd be here?" she hissed.

"Not at all. Ellen says you're planning a big bash for them."

"We haven't discussed any details yet."

He sipped his drink. "So which one of us is going to leave?"

"*I'm* not leaving. This is work." She turned up her powdered nose and looked everywhere in the room except at him. "After dinner, I'm sure a man with your skills can think of some excuse for your sudden departure."

He threw back his drink, then eyed her as she continued.

"An accident, maybe? Or a sickness in the family?"

"Or," he said, "I could stay and watch you worm your feminine wiles into the good senator's wallet."

"You mean, heart?"

"He doesn't have one."

"Well, you should know."

"What does *that* mean?"

"It takes one to know one." She spun away and in a few strides stood next to the senator. She smiled brightly, looping her arm through his. The senator leaned forward and whispered in her ear. A soft laugh escaped her lips.

Will tossed back the rest of his drink just as Ellen announced dinner.

* * *

Clare stared at the name on the place-setting card. She was seated next to Will. She glanced around the table as the others took their chairs. Pressing her lips together, she squared her shoulders and sat down.

She picked up her wineglass and took a sip.

"I thought you didn't drink?" Will said.

"I don't usually, but I find I need something, *anything* to dull the senses."

"Nice to know I have that effect."

"Don't flatter yourself. There are all kinds of reasons one may need to dull the senses. Snake bites for instance."

"Or, extreme disappointment in another?"

His remark hit home. For a second, guilt washed over her. A sudden onslaught of heat crept up her neck and onto her face. Probably too much to hope he hadn't noticed.

She turned her attention to the man on her right and made a point to engage him, but it seemed he was more interested in the redhead sitting to *his* right.

Will leaned over and whispered in her ear. "How awkward."

Clare pinned him with her most haughty expression. "Excuse me?"

"A woman with your assets being overlooked for a rather plump, little redhead." He sat back holding his wineglass between his fingers. "I bet you're not used to that."

"Well, we can't all be winners *all* the time. Take you, for instance. I imagine you've had your share of disappointments with the opposite sex."

He nodded. "I'll admit, there's some truth to that. I've had my share of narrow escapes from those who were only after my money. Women like you."

"Puleese," she scoffed.

"I call that being lucky."

"More like *un*lucky. Is it any wonder you're not married? A man who insults a woman for his own gain gets what he deserves."

The amusement in his eyes faded. His phone buzzed, and he glanced at the screen.

Her inner smirk screeched to a halt. What a cruel and thoughtless thing to say. She licked her suddenly dry lips. He was still focused on his phone.

Just as she opened her mouth to apologize, he pushed back from the table and stood, walked over to their hostess, and spoke a few quiet words to her.

Ellen's forehead creased with concern, then she stood and walked Will to the front door. Clare blinked and stared after him. Will snatched up his overnight bag, shook Ellen's hand, then left.

Go after him. Tell him you didn't mean it. She shot from her chair and rushed outside.

Will was just tossing his bag in the back seat of his Jag.

"Will, wait!"

He turned around just as she stopped in front of him.

"I'm sorry. That was a rotten thing to say. I'm a lot of things, but I'm never cruel. Please don't leave."

His lips quirked at the corners. "You think I'm leaving because of what you said?"

"Aren't you?"

He shook his head and lifted his cell phone. "I got a message from my board chairman. A business emergency. It's probably nothing too serious."

"Oh."

"So." A roguish twinkle appeared in his eyes. "I'll see you next week, then."

She sucked in an angry breath, pressed her hands against her thighs and nodded. He'd done that deliberately. Knowing she'd feel guilty. And like a fool, she'd fallen for it.

Chapter Sixteen

The fifty-four-foot cruiser sped across the blue gulf waters to Carrington Key Island. It sat twenty-two miles off Key West.

They docked at the pier closest to the main house. Sweat glistened off Will's tanned, muscular arms as he stooped to tie off the boat. In white jeans, a polo shirt, and docksides, he looked every bit the wealthy, thirty-something yacht owner and could have easily been shooting an ad for GQ Magazine.

He was undeniably one of the most gorgeous men she'd ever seen. For a moment she let her thoughts roam. A few weeks ago, they'd stood on the beach watching the sunset, with the promise of more to come.

She groaned inwardly. How could one kiss haunt her every waking moment? But it had. The wonderful feel of leaning against his chest had created an inner yearning for something far deeper. And God help her if he was the only person who could fulfill it. Regret tugged at her heart for what might have been.

"Come," he said. "The house is this way."

Will didn't wait, just strolled off expecting Clare to keep up.

Fine.

That worked for her. Better for her if he kept his distance. Not yet having lived down her humiliating exit from the previous weekend, she didn't need his undue attention while here. She'd get right to work with Mary and do her best to ignore him the rest of the weekend.

"Hello! Grandmother?" Will yelled. Silence. He strolled across the wide hall into the living room. He paused, then headed back into the hallway.

"She's a bit hard of hearing," he said.

As Clare followed him, she kept her eyes glued to his wide shoulders and slim hips.

He stopped in front of the sideboard hutch at the far end of the hallway. There was an envelope propped against the mirror. He slit it open and scanned the page. The distant drone of a boat engine feathered across her brain. Something was wrong.

"What is it?"

"It seems Granny's been called away."

She glared at him. "How convenient."

"I think so, too."

She should have known it was a trap. "Let me see that."

She snatched the note from his fingers. It was blank. "What kind of game are you playing?"

He folded his arms and pinned her to the floor with one look. "I could ask you the same question. So, Miss Clare Sullivan." He ambled with purpose toward her. She took a hasty step back. "I have no idea what that gold digger stunt was about, but this weekend, I mean to find out."

"You're kidnapping me?"

"Of course not. Feel free to leave anytime you want."

She pivoted and stalked toward the front door. She could tell he was following her. Just let him try and stop her.

Squinting against the bright sunlight, she marched back to the dock. When it came into view, she stopped. The boat was gone.

"I guess you'll have to swim for it."

She spun back around, his low chuckle infuriating her. "Where's the boat?"

"Gone."

"I can see that. But where is it?" A knot formed in the pit of her stomach. "We just left it here minutes ago."

"My groundskeeper had plans for it." Will's mocking smile taunted her.

"You can't keep me here. I'll report you to the police. I'll Facebook it. Tweet it. I'll ruin you and your coffee company. Don't think I won't."

"Be my guest." With that, he turned back toward the house, leaving her no choice but to follow.

She entered the house behind him. Her cases were gone. "Where're my things?"

"I texted Alphonse to take the bags I'd left in the foyer. Sorry sweetheart. They're gone, too."

"My laptop was in there. My life is on that computer."

"Don't worry. Your precious things will be safe and sound in my home office in Miami."

She snatched up her purse and pulled out her cell phone. No signal. She lifted angry eyes to his matter-of-fact gaze.

"I was never going to meet with your grandmother, was I?"

He shook his head. "I'm afraid not."

"And I suppose she's not the tyrant you led me to believe?"

"Oh, that part's true. And you'll be pleased to know, she'll have my hide when she finds out about this."

"That's something, I guess." She marched into the living room and sat down. "Fine. Go ahead. Take your pound of flesh and then call back the boat." She had the sudden urge to cry, but instead she clasped her hands together and stared ahead of her. And waited.

* * *

An expression of complete acceptance of doom crossed Clare's features, lending a certain vulnerability Will hadn't seen in her before. It caught him completely off guard. But only for a moment.

Nuh, uh. No way was he falling for that.

"I'm afraid I can't call the boat back," he said. "Alphonse's niece is getting married in Miami, and I specifically brought the boat here for him to use. His wife and daughter left in their boat yesterday."

She stood to her feet. "I'd like to freshen up, please."

"Of course. The bathroom is just off the kitchen. Right through there."

She breezed past him, heading in the direction he'd indicated. Never one to rush, Will took his time following her. Besides, he might as well enjoy the rear view of her lovely curves before the storm.

She passed through the hall, then turned right into the sprawling green and white kitchen.

"It's right through there," he said.

He made a point to wait for her. When she returned, they walked back to the living room.

"Have a seat. You look like you could use a drink." He splashed gold liquid into a glass and handed it to her.

"No, thank you," she said.

He shrugged. "Suit yourself." He sat down opposite her and crossed one leg over the other. Sipping his whiskey, he gave her look for look. "You know, I can do this all day *and* night."

"So what? Does that mean I'm not allowed to sleep while I'm here?"

"Of course you'll be allowed to sleep. As many nights here as it takes." He grinned, knowing full well it would infuriate her even more.

She raised her chin a fraction. "You're hateful. But with your history, I shouldn't be surprised."

"Finally, we seem to be getting somewhere. *And* we have a history?"

She dropped her gaze from his and stared at his chest.

"Please, enlighten me?" While he waited for a response, he swirled the tumbler in his hand, causing the ice cube to clink against the glass.

Her long lashes fluttered against her cheek, making her appear nervous, which he highly doubted.

"Why don't you just spit it out?" he said. "While I'm in a listening mood."

She raised her eyes to his. "I have something to say to you, all right. But *I* will pick the time and the place to do it."

"Ah, a woman who takes control. I like that."

Her sparkling eyes clouded with doubt and uncertainty. She was finding him hard to read. For the moment, that suited him just fine. A woman with her designs needed to be kept on her toes. Poetic justice, as he'd had to learn the art of being unreadable because of women like her.

"Okay," he said. "I'll start." He set his tumbler on the side table, never taking his eyes from her face. "You've disliked me from the first day I met you. Like most men, I have the hunter instinct. And you, my dear Miss Sullivan, with your glittering, green, accusatory eyes, tossed me a dare I frankly couldn't ignore. And whether you believe it or not, what you said to me was 'come and get me.'"

Her expressive eyes flared.

"I did no such thing. I wanted nothing to do with you. You two-faced, arrogant..." She looked him up and down. "You and your hurtful, callous words."

Clare puffed up, reminding him of a threatened parrot.

He stared at her, dumbfounded as to what she could be talking about. This was getting more and more interesting. He picked up his glass and eyed it. "To my recollection, I've seldom, if *ever* been the callous type."

"You know what they say." She shrugged. "If the shoe fits."

Her sassy, bravado act came across purely as self-preservation, and there was something poignant in that. What was it about her that could both irritate and tug on his heartstrings all at the same time?

She blinked and glanced toward the door.

"Waiting for reinforcements?"

Her eyes widened a fraction.

"I thought so." He shook his head. "No one's coming. It's just you and me."

She scowled and squeezed her fists. "I knew I shouldn't have trusted you."

"If you aren't ready to talk. That's fine." He threw back a portion of his drink and stretched out his legs, crossing one ankle over the other. "I'm in no hurry."

She stared at him with those expressive eyes of hers, all appealing and scrumptious. Everything he'd ever wanted in a woman. When he'd imagined bringing her to his family estate, he'd hoped to introduce her to his grandmother and his brothers as someone more than just a friend.

There was now no doubt, she'd had it out for him from the very beginning. He simply hadn't wanted to see it. More fool him.

Still. He adored this woman. This deceiving, maddening, and heaven help him, adorable woman. And if he had anything to say about it, they were not leaving here until he found out the truth. Was she gold or pyrite?

Chapter Seventeen

There was something quite heady about being kid-napped. Clare's thoughts sailed over the many romance novels she'd read as a teenager. The gorgeous, all-male, dark-haired pirate. The innocent heroine, flung over his shoulder, while he climbed the rope ladder up the side of a great sailing ship.

She gazed at her captor lazing comfortably on the chair opposite, eyeing her over the rim of his whiskey tumbler as if he had all the time in the world.

With his dark hair and ocean blue eyes that held a humorous, almost devilish twinkle, she grudgingly admitted, he was rather swoon-worthy. But aside from that, he was no hero. His distasteful words at Lenny's sandwich shop still appalled her.

She'd come close to confessing why she'd decorated his condo in the gold rush theme. But, keeping him dangling was just too delicious. He was mistaken if he thought she was going to cave and spill all. He was certainly shocked at her recent accusation. He actually had no idea what she was talking about.

Good. Let him wonder. Let him squirm. Let him feel the pain of ruthless words for a change.

"So. You own an island," she said.

"Are you sure you don't want something to drink?"

"Mr. Carrington, are you hoping to get me drunk?"

"You must really think the worst of me." He stood and gazed down at her. "But there's water, tea, and coffee, if you're interested."

"Fine. I'll take a water."

He grabbed a chilled bottle of spring water from the bar fridge, walked back to her chair, then handed it to her.

"Would you like a tour of the grounds before dark?"

Now what was he up to? She chewed on her inside lip, then shrugged. "Sure, then maybe you can tell me more about your island. It is yours, right? I mean, we're not tres-passing or anything, are we?"

"And if we were?" His eyes mocked.

He was baiting her.

"Just something else I can report to the police."

Lush, tropical gardens greeted her as they stepped out back. The maintenance alone would be a full-time job. The sleek, rectangular swimming pool off the back terrace with a pool house sitting opposite created a lovely compound effect.

"I could spend all my time right here," she said as they strolled through the intimate cabana area. The heady scent of gardenia and jasmine permeated the air.

As they paused at the pool's edge, she took a swig from the water bottle and looked around. Palm trees of all types graced the seating area and thick, colorful annuals spilled from massive, well-placed stone pots.

"Look." Will pointed toward the ocean. A school of porpoises swam right off the shore, their back fins arching through the water.

"I love that," she said. For a moment everything was wonderful. Will Carrington's warm and thoughtful actions over the past two months came soaring to the surface.

Had she misjudged him? She glanced at his profile. He was still looking out to sea. A hint of a smile played about his firm lips. His eyes held warmth and interest in the view. This was the face she'd seen so often. She'd wanted to believe this was the real Will Carrington, but every time she started to, the memory of his cruel words would taunt her. Confusing. Frustrating. And disappointing.

As for her. When had she become so vindictive? Why did she feel the need to keep score? She wasn't an ugly, hateful person. He was darned attractive and secretly, she'd wanted to fix him, fix the situation. There was so much to like about Will Carrington. Why couldn't she focus on that?

"Penny for them." He was still gazing at the ocean and yet he'd known she was looking at him.

Clare blinked, then shook her head. "I was thinking how amazing they are." She nodded toward the porpoises. "How in tune they seem to be to each other. No fighting, no worrying, no angst. Just being in the moment. Being what God created them to be."

She raised her eyes to his. Will was looking at her as if he couldn't quite figure her out.

"Really?" His lips quirked a heart-stopping smile. "I could have sworn you were looking at me."

"Kiss me, Will."

She held back a smile at Will's dumbfounded expression.

"What?"

"*Kiss* me."

His eyes narrowed. "Is this a trick question."

"No." She moved forward until she was inches from his rugged face.

A deep twinkle appeared in his eyes. "I have to say, I've thought of nothing else for the last, oh I don't know, month." He slipped the water bottle from her fingers and set it on the table near his hip.

"Then what are you waiting for?" She raised her face to his. She felt the warmth of his breath before his lips feathered hers. Gentle, questioning. Barely touching.

"Don't worry," she whispered. "I don't bite."

"I'm not too sure about that."

Clare's stomach plummeted at the hunger and need in Will's eyes. No man had ever looked at her like that. She had no idea he'd wanted her this much.

As his lips moved to claim hers, she angled her head to the side with a desire to tease. After all, his kind only took in order to satisfy their own needs.

But then, his lips caressed her cheek with a sweetness she'd never experienced. Startled, she wasn't quite sure what to do with this gentle feathering, exploration of her neck and…

Oh.

Dear.

Lord…her shoulder. In spite of her plan to turn the tables, she arched against him. His mouth brushed teasing strokes down the center of her chest toward her breasts.

He lifted his head, and she moaned.

Don't stop. As if he could read her thoughts, his lips covered hers.

Pirate lips.

Stealing.

Plundering that which he did not own.

Overwhelmed, she placed her hands against his chest and pushed. She sucked in a deep, controlling breath. He immediately released her.

Gasping, she stepped back, then turned and raced back to the house.

* * *

Will raked his hand over the back of his neck and waited for his beating heart to slow down.

God, he wanted to go on kissing her. He wanted so much more. His need for her overshadowed all else. He'd known for weeks that he loved her, but past experience had taught him to be careful with his heart.

In his younger days he'd fallen so easily. Played the fool. Over the last ten years he'd learned to temper his emotions where women were concerned. Women who'd used his kind and goodhearted soul for their financial benefit. Wes had just *used* them back, but he couldn't be like his brother. So he kept his distance, telling himself that the next time he fell in love it would be real and lasting. Even with all her mystery, he thought he'd found that in Clare.

When he got back to the house, she was in the kitchen standing in front of the refrigerator door. "What've you planned for dinner?"

He gazed at her. "I... Are you okay?"

She stood straight-backed and poised. "Of course."

He nodded, continuing to eye her. Cool, calm, and collected.

Light slowly dawned, and he wanted to kick himself. Man she was good. *Dammit.* Like a fool, he'd fallen right in with her little plan.

Well, I have plans for you, too, Miss Sullivan. Tonight couldn't come soon enough.

Chapter Eighteen

"I have several things ready for the oven," Will said. "I'll take care of it, and you can go freshen up if you'd like."

"Thank you."

"I'll show you to the guest room." They mounted the stairs in silence. "Here you are."

Clare stood at the door and glanced around. A mixture of cool blues and greens welcomed her as she entered the room.

"You should find everything you need here and in the bathroom. Dinner will be served in one hour." He pulled the door closed, then left.

Will entered the kitchen. He set the oven for 350 degrees, then slid each covered dish onto the middle shelf. After setting the timer for forty-five minutes, he made his way back to Clare's room.

Placing his ear against the door, he could hear the shower running. He gently turned the doorknob and peeked inside the bedroom. He found Clare's blouse and shorts on the club chair in the corner and quickly snatched them up. As he turned to leave, he noticed her bra and panties, grinned, and took them as well.

He crossed the hall to his room, showered, and got dressed. As he tucked his white-collared shirt into his dress slacks, he wondered what Clare's reaction would be when she saw the dress. He'd only provided one outfit for the evening. If she refused to wear it, well...

He spotted his reflection in the mirror and laughed. "You really should *not* be this happy."

When he got to the kitchen, the aroma of beef tenderloin and seasoned potatoes permeated the room. He grabbed an oven mitt and went to work. After he had each plate filled, he set them under the stove heat lamps, then waited.

* * *

Clare stood in front of the open closet and gasped. An old west, saloon-hall dress hung all alone in the center of the closet. She recognized it from the theme party. The gold-sequined, snug-fitting bodice and the gauzy red skirt screamed floozy of the highest order.

She grabbed the dress, angling it for a better look. Low cut and completely backless, with only spaghetti straps to hold it in place. Something she'd never wear.

She looked around for her shorts and top. They were nowhere to be found.

"Why that no good—" She sucked in a strangled breath. "He even took my underwear?" She cinched the bath towel tighter, spun back around to face the closet, then glanced up.

Two gauzy-bowed, gold boxes, one round and the other square, sat conspicuously on the top shelf. She grimaced as she reached up on tiptoe to pull them down.

Setting them on the foot of the bed, she pulled one end of the ribbon on the smaller box and lifted the lid. Her jaw dropped. A pair of red lace panties mocked from the surrounding tissue. She sucked in a slow breath, then opened the bandbox. She reached in and pulled out a red felt hat adorned with flamboyant yellow plums. Seething, she threw the hat back in the box, knowing it was no more than she deserved.

Twenty minutes later, Clare strolled past Mary's bedroom and spotted a lacy shawl lying over the back of a floral-covered chair. She snatched it up, threw it over her shoulders and headed for the dining room. She took her time, ambling through the house, pausing now and again to enjoy some of the many paintings throughout the large home. When she arrived at the entrance, she stopped and stared. The lights were low, and candles flickered over the china and crystal-laden table.

Will's back was to her. When he turned, his eyes displayed admiration and appreciation. Gone was the mocking humor from earlier.

Clare placed her hands on her hips. "Okay. I'll play along."

"Careful how you say that. After this afternoon, I *could* get the wrong impression."

As she stood in the doorway, he scanned her with a head-to-toe glance that tingled her flesh. Then with a flourish, he pulled out a chair.

"Dinner is ready." He motioned to the chair. "Please, sit."

Her skirt swished as she approached the table. Thankfully, the noise stopped when she sat down.

"Here. I'll take that." He lifted the shawl off her shoulders and tossed it on the chair to his right.

It was all she could do not to throw her hands over her cleavage. Vulnerable and half-naked did not sit well with her. At all.

"I hope you like beef." He lifted the silver domes from the plates releasing the juicy scent of hot beef and buttered biscuits.

"This looks divine." She inhaled slowly, regaining her poise. "I didn't know you could cook like this."

"I can't. Sophie, Alphonse's wife, prepared it for the weekend. She's an amazing cook."

She cut a portion of meat and placed it in her mouth. It was good. Delicious, in fact. Until that moment, Clare hadn't realized how hungry she was.

A companionable silence settled over the room as they ate, with the occasional clink of fork against china.

Clare reached for her wineglass, paused, and took hold of the water instead. She wouldn't drink while she was here. It was important she keep her wits about her. His gorgeous, GQ Magazine looks and the deep timbre of his voice made her dizzy enough without adding alcohol to the mix.

"Don't you like reds?"

Her eyes met his. In the candlelight they had darkened to a deep blue. She wondered what the candlelight was doing to her own eyes right at this moment. Wondered if he saw her in a new or different light.

"I lean more to the whites."

He stood. "That can easily be rectified."

Rectified? Boy, oh boy, is he good.

He was playing a part, from his black riverboat gambler suit to his formal speech.

"That's really not necessary. I'm not going to drink while I'm on this island."

There. She said it. It was out. Her weakness. She all but admitted self-control around him would be difficult, if not *impossible*, if she drank.

He sat back down and stretched out his long legs in front of him, crossing them at the ankles.

She reached for her water, trying her best not to let his scrutiny rattle her. She forced herself to look at him, and she immediately regretted it. Dang if he couldn't look right through her like a cougar on the hunt.

She blinked and licked her lips. An action which refocused his piercing gaze.

"What's for dessert?" Her heart raced, and she wondered if this was how a scared rabbit felt.

* * *

Will loved it when a plan came together, and this one was flowing along beautifully. So well in fact, if he wasn't careful, Clare might be inclined to get up and run. And that wouldn't fit in with his plans at all.

And if she gnaws any more on her bottom lip, there won't be much left to kiss.

He held out his arms. "Come here."

Her eyes widened, and her jaw dropped two inches.

"In your dreams."

"There *is* some truth to that." He made a deliberate show of getting out of his chair, and an equally deliberate one of removing his jacket and tie.

After tossing both on the back of his chair, he took a step in her direction.

"What are you doing?" Alarm filled her eyes.

"Getting comfortable and finishing what you started this afternoon." He undid the top button on his dress shirt, then the next. "Do you mind?"

"Yes, I mind." She shot to her feet, snatched up the shawl and held it to her chest. "This has gone far enough."

He shook his head. "Not nearly." He stopped in front of her, gave her the slightest of smiles, then scooped her up in his arms as if she were a child.

She sucked in a breath and push hard against his chest. "Put me down."

"That's the plan, sweetheart. The question is, where?"

She stiffened, and her lovely eyes darkened. With her slender form secured tightly against his chest, he strode from the dining room, then across the wide hall into the living room. She held herself perfectly still until he sat on the sofa, where she proceeded to push even harder.

"Struggling will only make this last a lot longer. If that's your intent, it's perfectly fine with me. I like you here."

Her chest heaved, and he laughed. "Admit it. You're enjoying this as much as I am."

"You're a bully."

He grinned, intent on infuriating her even more. "I rather enjoy having you in my arms. But seriously, I'm surprised at you. A gold digger with your experience, struggling and carrying on like you're some sweet innocent, when we both know you're not."

He banded his arms tightly around her and waited. He could and *would* outlast her.

She glared at him. "You really think I'm after your money?"

"Well, when I consider the recent and extreme change in your wardrobe and the flaunting of the diamond bracelet, thing... It's kind of hard not to. Besides, isn't that what you wanted me to think?"

She opened her kissable mouth then clamped it shut.

"But then..." He gave her a hint of a smile. "I nixed that notion when you ran after me the other night."

She sucked air through her clenched teeth. "Then what?"

"There're all kinds of gold diggers, and they're not all after money. For example, *position* is high on the list. Like in a company or in society. Some, and this is where I think you fit in, are seeking revenge, or possibly payback. This young lady is not really a gold digger, in the true sense, but she uses the idea to take the unsuspecting male off the scent, as it were. Sort of a bait and switch."

She dropped her gaze from his.

"Am I getting warm?"

Finally, to his enormous relief, she relaxed. That is, if not straining against him with all of her physical strength could be called relaxing. At least she'd stopped fighting him, but her breathing was still hard, making her breasts rise and fall. Her face flushed the prettiest pink, but her eyes sparked daggers.

"Are we through?"

She didn't answer. Just sat straining against his banded arms, leaning back as far away from him as possible.

"I'm not a fool," she said. "I'll admit I'm not as strong as you. But don't think for one second that weakness extends to anything beyond the physical."

"I'll take that as a *yes*." He loosened his hold, but still kept his arms securely around her. "Now, I think it's time for some answers. But first, dessert."

He lowered his head to kiss her. She drew back, and his gaze locked with hers. He had one rule. Never kiss a woman unless it was mutual. Clare would not be an exception. He'd wait until either her eyes or her mouth said yes.

So he lingered over her, allowing his eyes to roam free. From the loose tendrils at her hairline, to her moist, slightly parted lips. He knew his desire was raw, and if she only realized it, hers for the taking.

Something close to panic filled her eyes. Was it possible this pent-up, professional-turned vamp didn't have that much experience with men? There was only one way to find out.

He continued to hold her and waited for some sign, some *inkling* that he should continue. He'd never known a woman who could tie him in such knots. Clare Sullivan was that woman.

In the month he'd known her, he'd come to believe she had real feelings for him. If she didn't know how he felt about her after this, then she never would.

Longing filled her eyes, desire etched her face, eradicating any angst from earlier. She inched toward him, and that's all the invitation he needed.

His lips covered hers.

Determined to melt her distrusting little heart, he wound his fingers through the supple curls of her hair, fisting the silky strands while adding pressure to her bare back with his other hand.

Even though she still held herself somewhat rigid, her tentative, uncertainty was sweetness itself. He grazed his lips along her cheek, to her smooth tense jaw, until a tender moan escaped her mouth.

Sweet victory.

She gripped his shoulders. His heart quickened. He could almost taste it, but it was short-lived. She pushed against his chest, as if she'd come to her senses.

"We shouldn't," she whispered, uncertainty and passion spilling from her eyes.

"We *should.*" His eyes bore into hers as he stroked the hair from her forehead, speaking softly, but pointedly.

Then while keeping one arm securely around her, he lowered her to the sofa, her slender body warm and pliable beneath him. Tenderly, he kissed one side of her mouth, then the other. "You're so, so beautiful." Impossible to hold himself in check any longer, he claimed her mouth in his need for her. Fervently. Hungrily.

She gripped his shoulders, then slid her hands along his back. Eager and exploring. His heart soared at the feel of her, all but scorching his flesh through his cotton shirt.

Her hands faltered, a soft whimper escaped her lips, then she kissed him fully, finally surrendering. Her response lit a fire in his belly, and he pressed against her. Honey dripped from her lips. In his whole life he would never get enough of her.

Her heart raced beneath him, ratcheting his pulse up a notch. It tattooed a sweet rhythm through a sea of sequins pulled tautly against her breasts. The image of a frightened rabbit rose in his mind. He pulled back, suddenly uncertain.

"Am I going too fast?"

Her swollen lips trembled. It was all he could do not to reclaim them. The sleepy, passionate gleam in her glowing eyes pleaded with him not to stop. This was not the face of an experienced lover. And certainly not that of a vamp or a gold digger. The face staring so appealingly up at him held desire.

Oh God, could it be something more?

He sat up and for a moment just stared at her. He groaned inwardly at the sudden faltering in her countenance, the lowering of her eyes. Disappointment and something akin to horror covered her face. She blinked back tears and pushed herself to a seated position.

"You're right." He ran his hand over the back of his neck. "This has gone far enough."

She glanced away, refusing to look at him. He grabbed the lightweight shawl off the floor, looped it over her shoulders, then tied it under her chin.

She raised searching eyes to his face.

"You're way too tempting the other way."

"Well, aren't you suddenly all gallant," she bit out, pulling the shawl closer.

He'd hurt her feelings. Regret filled him. *That* he hadn't planned on.

"Even us cavemen have our moments. Or, would you prefer I have no self-control?"

She pressed her fingers against her recently kissed lips and stared back at him.

He stood, holding out his hand. "How about some coffee?"

Her gaze dropped from his face to his hand. Then like a feral cat, afraid to trust, she stood without taking it.

"We'll have that chat." He grabbed her hand anyway and pulled her alongside him to the kitchen, thankful she didn't resist. If she had, then he would have had to carry her, would have had to feel her beating heart against his own, her warm breath against his neck. And there was no telling where that would have led. He was certain of one thing, though. He wouldn't have been able to stop himself a second time.

* * *

Will flicked on the kitchen lights and motioned Clare to a chair. She cinched the shawl around her shoulders and watched him. In two strides, he was in front of the counter making coffee.

The kitchen was bright all right, and it may be quelling his amorous spirit, but she wasn't sure if it would quiet hers. To say she was disappointed when he stopped kissing her was an understatement. More like, *crushed.*

Her heart and mind had cried out for him to continue. But her mouth would never have uttered the sentiment out loud. In all of her twenty-six years, she'd never experienced such a longing. True, she'd had little experience with men when it came to the physical. She'd made her choice long ago, so she wasn't complaining, but a little experience sure would've come in handy about ten minutes ago.

Was it her lack of experience that had made him stop? Humiliation pumped through her veins at the mere thought. Megan already had more dates then Clare had ever had. She wasn't sure which was worse, her lack of ex-perience, or that she'd fallen for this self-assured, arrogant, womanizer. Raw ache filled her heart. She knew in that moment, she could never let him know.

She gazed at his broad back and lean hips and swallowed. The sensation of his powerful, relentless hold over her still tingled her flesh. As if he'd staked his claim and she belonged to no one else.

And what if love were attached to that kind of possessive passion? The thought taunted, and she knew it would be heavenly. She sucked in a steadying breath and could kick herself for being attracted to him. She clamped her teeth over her lower lip. And if kisses could kill, she'd be a dead woman for certain.

She glanced around the kitchen. This would be a good time to throw something, but Clare Sullivan didn't throw tantrums *or* things.

Will set the coffee tray on the table. "There's cream and sugar if you want."

"Black is fine." She lifted the hot mug to her lips and sipped.

He heaved a sigh, and she raised her eyes to his.

"Who are you, Clare? Won't you please tell me?"

The weary catch in Will's voice caught her off guard.

"It's a simple question," he said.

"I'm afraid the answer could take all night." Heat crept up her cheeks, and she hastily took another sip, scalding her lip in the process. She winced, placing her free hand to her mouth.

"That shouldn't be a problem since we have all weekend." His eyes twinkled, and it was obvious he was still enjoying this game of cat and mouse.

"I'm Clare Sullivan. I'm a designer, and I live in Naples, Florida. I've been—"

"Careful, I might start kissing you again."

"Male dominance to the rescue. Is that it? The only way for you to get your way?"

"It does come in handy." He grinned. "Especially with beautiful gold-seeking fortune hunters."

She raised her chin. The last thing she needed was for him to start kissing her again.

She'd be lost.

A goner.

Better for him to keep thinking she was after his money.

She ran her finger around the lip of the mug, then raised her eyes to his. "I do so like pretty things." She fluttered her lashes and smiled.

He pressed his lips together and shook his head.

"Fine," she said. "What about a question that won't take all night to answer?"

"Fair enough." He spooned sugar into his cup and stirred. "Who did I hurt?" He sat back in his chair, his eyes serious, his face solemn.

Her heart plummeted to her stomach. At least he admitted to hurting others. She gripped her mug.

"Come on. I must have hurt someone close to you for you to go to such lengths, for what? Revenge? So, who? A former lover?"

"I don't have any former lovers." *Oh gosh, did she just say that out loud?*

He leaned forward. "Somehow, I find that hard to believe," he whispered.

She drummed her fingers against the table top and gave him her 'look'. The one she'd used several hundred times with Megan.

A crooked smile creased his face. "An old boyfriend, then. I've wracked my brain trying to figure it out."

"Who says it was a man?"

"Now we're getting somewhere. See. That wasn't so hard." He rubbed his chin. "So, it's a woman." He sipped his coffee. "That actually makes sense."

Her skin prickled. "You seem quite cavalier about it. Which doesn't surprise me in the least."

"Really? You think you know me?" He shrugged. "I admit, I have kicked a few women in their delightful rear ends and would gladly do it again. Any woman who leads a man to believe it's his love and affection they desire, only to reveal it's his money they wanted all along, deserves a swift kick in their form-fitting designer jeans."

So someone in his past had led him on. Used him for what she could get. Clare could see why he'd be on alert where a younger sibling was concerned, but then, so was she.

He stood to his feet and towered over her, clearly frustrated that the conversation wasn't going as he'd planned.

She licked her lips. "You asked the question. And I answered it," she said. "I'm sorry it wasn't the answer you wanted."

"You're right. I think it *is* time for you to go. Unfortunately, that won't be possible until Alphonse returns with my boat on Sunday." An outrageous twinkle filled his eyes. "I'm afraid you and I will just have to *tolerate* one another until then. Good night, Miss Sullivan."

Back straight, he strode from the room, leaving her sitting at the kitchen table.

* * *

Taffeta and crepe swished against Clare's legs as she mounted the steps that led to her bedroom. She'd have to get her shorts back in the morning. No way would she wear this costume the entire weekend. She wondered what size his grandmother wore. Anything was preferable to crepe and sequins.

Suddenly tired, she undressed, then climbed between the sheets. She pulled the covers to her chin, feeling completely naked, and it wasn't because she hadn't a stitch on. She'd been a fool to play into his lovemaking tactics. He'd made her feel vulnerable and exposed.

She groaned and punched the pillow underneath her head. Earlier, she'd flung the sequined dress across the corner chair. But in the lateness of the hour, the sequins mocked from across the room. It was her own fault she was in this situation.

She turned her back to the dress, closed her eyes, and pulled the sheet tighter. A sudden knock, then another echoed from the other side of the closed door. Her eyes flew wide open.

"Don't you *dare* open that door," she wailed.

The knob turned, then a small crack appeared. To her horror, Will poked his head inside.

She yanked the sheet even higher. "Get out."

"I just thought you might want this." He held up an ankle-length cotton nightgown. "But..." He shrugged and started to leave.

"Wait. Yes. I...just leave it right by the door and go."

Amusement filled his gorgeous eyes, and she wanted to slap him. She lay perfectly still until he closed the door. She held her breath and waited. The thought that he might open the door as soon as her feet hit the floor pinned her to the mattress.

One, two... When she reached ten, she threw off the covers, jumped from the bed, then snatched the gown off the floor. Safely back under the covers with the gown clutched to her chest, she quickly slipped the mass of white cotton over her head, then fell against the pillow in a warm sweat.

"And here's Granny's matching robe."

Clare sat up with a jerk.

Will sailed in, then tossed the robe on the foot of the bed. "Mornings can be chilly." His eyes gleamed with humor as he turned away.

She picked up a pillow, then threw it, hitting him squarely in the back. A deep chuckle escaped his lips as he closed the door again.

She stormed from the bed, covers flying. She yanked the desk chair from under the writing desk, lugged it across the carpet, then jammed it under the doorknob with a final push. "That should take care of any more intrusions."

But later, as she lay on her side, she smiled dreamily, wondering what else Will may have in store for her.

Chapter Nineteen

Clare awoke to the smell of bacon and coffee.

She sat up, drew her knees to her chest, and glanced around the room. Her gaze fell on the door, and she sucked in a sharp breath. The chair she'd secured under the handle was not only gone, but it was back under the desk on the opposite wall.

She threw off the covers and slid from the bed. Her shorts and blouse were on the corner chair, and her suitcase sat on a stand at the foot of the bed.

Fists on hips, she stepped to the wall behind the desk. It was paneled in white-washed wood. Feeling a bit silly, she pressed on the panels to see if any one of them would open, but they didn't.

Next she tried the closet. Stepping inside, she felt along the bare walls, behind the shelves, then the corners. Nothing. She gnawed her bottom lip. There had to be a way in here. It would have been impossible to move that chair otherwise.

She stood in the middle of the room and scanned the ceiling. What was she missing? Squatting down, she flipped the corners of the rug back to check the floorboards. Still nothing.

After she brushed her teeth, she slipped on Granny's robe and went downstairs.

* * *

Will was just pouring his second cup of coffee when Clare entered the kitchen. "Sleep well?"

"I did. Especially after I secured the door with the desk chair. You?"

"Better than ever." He hid his smile. No one had ever been able to find the secret door to that room. He and Wes had played many pranks on past houseguests when they were younger. "Coffee?"

"Please." Clare sat primly at the table. Her eyes followed him from one side of the counter to the other reminding him of one of those scenes in horror films where the eyes watch you from the ancestral portrait.

Last night she'd looked like dessert sitting up in the bed. Like a beautifully wrapped package begging to be opened. Boy, did he have it bad. He handed her a cup, then grabbed his plate.

"I hope you're hungry. I've prepared a big breakfast. Everything's on the stove, so help yourself." He placed a dinner-size plate filled with fried eggs, grits, bacon, and biscuits in front of him and sat down.

Clare walked to the stove, then picked up her plate. She was beautiful in the mornings without makeup. Her hair was piled on top of her head giving him a clear view of her profile. He thought of kissing her slender neck and the tiny space just behind her ear. He'd missed that spot yesterday and made a mental note not to next time. His grandmother's gown flowed around her bare ankles drawing attention to her feminine feet and coral painted toes. She even made Granny's gown look sexy.

She sat back down and paused when she realized he was watching her. She turned up her nose, flicking her napkin in her lap as she did so. He smiled and wished like the devil he could postpone Alphonse's return until Monday. "So, is this what you call *tolerating* each other?" She gazed at him with a big doe-eyed expression. "A gargantuan breakfast and a table set for two?" She jabbed a forkful of cheese grits into her pretty mouth and chewed, never taking her eyes off his face.

He grinned. She had to be dying to know how he got into her room.

"Forgive me." He placed his hand over his heart. "I seem to have lapsed into a hospitable moment. Tomorrow, you can fix your own breakfast."

She shrugged. "Oh, don't get me wrong. I'm enjoying the hospitality. And, may I remind you, it wasn't me who said we'd *tolerate* each other."

"So, you'd like to spend *more* time with me."

"Don't flatter yourself." She buttered a biscuit and took a bite. "Do you mind if I explore your island while I'm...*incarcerated* against my will?" She faked a smile to make her point.

"Not at all. The house, the grounds, any place you'd like to go is fine." He pushed his chair back and stood. "After you clean the kitchen."

She gaped at him and blinked. "Of course." She dabbed her mouth with a napkin. "That's only fair." She stood and started clearing the table.

"Great." He nodded. "I'll see you around."

* * *

The kitchen seemed unusually quiet after Will left. She'd be lying if she didn't admit to being disappointed. After such a meal and the fact that he went to so much trouble, she didn't think he really meant they'd spend the weekend just tolerating each other. She ran her fingers over her mouth where last night's kisses still lingered. She sighed and rinsed the plates and coffee mugs, then secured them in the dishwasher.

After finishing the clean-up, she went back to her room and quickly changed into shorts and a sleeveless silk blouse. Minutes later, she was outside with her face turned toward the sun. It was a gorgeous, sparkling day and darn it, she was going to enjoy it.

The grounds were beautifully maintained with curvy pathways throughout the lush surroundings. She chose the one that led to the beach.

She loved her walks along the shore in Naples, and today, she found herself meandering along the water's edge as if it were an ordinary Saturday. *I wonder what Megan's doing?* She let out a long sigh. *I wish I could call her.* Both Megan and Edward knew she was going away for the weekend with a client to work on a design, so at least they wouldn't be worried about her.

She'd been walking about thirty minutes, when she noticed a path up ahead. As she took the next curve, the path widened, leading to a quaint yellow cottage about a hundred yards from shore. Green plantation shutters flanked the front windows encased in empty flower boxes.

Never one to resist a tour, she picked her way across the low dunes to the front door and knocked. When no one answered, she peeked in the window and could tell it was uninhabited.

She turned the door handle and stepped inside.

Even though it was empty, the cottage was charm itself. It would be a perfect retreat for someone. Walking through the compact space, ideas flew at her like rice at a wedding. This must be the one Will's grandmother wanted her to fix up? She sat down in a small stuffed chair and fingered the well-worn fabric. She stared at the walls, wishing she had paper and pen, but her mental notes would have to suffice. She sat for some time envisioning what she could do with the place, then took one more walk through before going back outside.

She meandered around the structure, then looked left. The back of the main house was some distance away. She glanced at her watch, surprised to see it was already twelve-thirty, so she headed back to fix lunch.

After rinsing the sand from her feet, she entered the back door, into a wide hallway, then passed the laundry/mud-room before she found the kitchen.

She stopped at the entry. Will was already making him-self a sandwich.

"Mind if I join you?" She had a sudden urge to mess with him.

"Not at all."

"I was hoping to make you lunch, but I see you beat me to it."

He had a mouthful and all he could do was nod.

She made herself a sandwich, then eyed the chairs at the small dinette. Despite five chairs to choose from, she chose the one right next to him and sat down. A man with his level of arrogance and confidence didn't need a lot of per-sonal space, did he? She gave him her brightest smile, then dove into her ham and Swiss on rye.

Eying her, he took a swig of iced tea. "Cozy?"

"Uh huh," she said between bites.

He turned part way and placed his hand on his hip.

She stopped chewing, then swallowed. "I'm sorry. Am I bothering you?"

"There are six chairs at this table."

She sniffed, got up, and moved to the chair across from him. "Better?"

"Much." He took a huge bite of his sandwich and ignored her. He focused on his meal, refusing to look at her the entire time. In fact, she'd never seen anyone eat so quickly.

Good. The sooner he finished, the sooner he'd leave.

Sure enough, after shoving the last bite into his mouth, he got up, rinsed his plate, then headed for the door.

She watched him depart with a sense of elation. Her instinct was to hurry in the opposite direction. Instead, she finished her meal, knowing it would take that long to put some distance between them.

When she placed her empty plate in the sink next to his, she heard his footsteps echoing down the back steps. She'd clean up later. It was now time to continue exploring the island. Not for one second did she believe there wasn't another way off.

She slipped out the side door and hurried across the lush grounds toward the water. From there she'd make her way around the island and hopefully find a way off.

Just as she started to take the path leading to the ocean, she spotted Will seated under an umbrella at the pool's edge. He was looking right at her. She glanced longingly toward the gulf. Her exploration would have to wait until later.

She sauntered over to the pool area, deliberately pausing to smell the flowers along the way.

"I don't know who your landscapers are, but they've done a beautiful job." She threw her hand over one of the flower beds. "I love how they've combined this jumbled, haphazard mass of color within a definite structure."

Will peeled his tall self from the lounge chair as she approached. "My landscaper calls it chaotic organization."

"Right. That's exactly what it is." She stopped in front of him.

"It seems your creative abilities go toward gardening as well."

"They're similar, I guess." She shrugged. "But believe me, I've no green thumb."

She glanced up at him and caught her breath. His glowing eyes held her spellbound. He took one step, closing the gap between them, and placed his hands on her shoulders. Her heart stopped. She licked her suddenly dry lips.

He lifted his hands to the side of her face. "Are you following me?"

"Of course not. I was on my way to the beach and saw you. But if you're serious about keeping your distance, then I'll certainly—"

He covered her mouth with his. Sweet Jasmine filled her senses. And she knew, from that moment on, she'd forever link the two.

His warm lips seemed to tease and question all at the same time. The answer was a resounding *yes*. Whatever he wanted.

She linked her arms around his waist and melted against him. Kissing Will Carrington was heady, euphoric. Everything she'd ever dreamed a kiss could be. Ever since he'd kissed her on the beach in Naples, she'd longed to have him do it again, and last night's kiss had ended way too soon.

He didn't know it, but that had been her first *real* kiss. In her teen years everyone hung out in groups, then after her parents' death she'd stopped doing even that. No boyfriends, no kissing. At least not like this. This was the kiss dreams were made of.

But it was a lie. Everything he'd said at Lenny's flooded her dizzy brain. Her eyes flew open.

She planted her hands against his chest and pushed hard. As he released her, he lost his balance. Teetering on the edge of the pool, he threw out his arms to right himself.

"Oh, no." Clare gasped, wide-eyed, and reached for him.

Will clasped his hand in hers. But it was too late. As the heavier of the two, Will flailed backward and landed in the water, taking her with him.

Clare shrieked and tumbled forward, landing beside him. Water engulfed her. One second. Two seconds. She popped up and gulped air.

Will emerged and slung his head to the side.

Soaking wet, they stood facing each other in the shallow end. She hastily glanced at her chest. Her silk blouse clung to her like a second skin.

He peeled off his T-shirt and tossed it to the edge of the pool, then brushed the dampness from his eyes and forehead and gave her a teasing once over. "We might as well make the most of this." He waded toward her. "It's obvious my efforts to ignore you aren't working."

He stopped just short of touching her. He was so close she had to lean back to look at him.

"Most men in my position would say I deserve a medal for keeping my hands off you for as long as I have."

With only inches between them, Clare's stomach fluttered with wild butterflies. So this was what it was like to feel your heart pound with such force you were certain it would burst. To be totally and completely overwhelmed with the heady scent of pure maleness.

He was beautiful, having just been dunked. Afternoon sunlight bounced off the pool water making him look all Greek god and gorgeous. He gazed at her through his long, wet lashes as if trying to read her.

Aching like a hormonal teenager, she lowered her eyes to his bare chest. What would it hurt to let go, just this once? Tentatively placing her right hand on his glistening shoulder, she splayed her fingers across his flesh, then snatched them away as if he were on fire.

"God, Clare. Do you have any idea what you're doing to me?"

"I... Are you trying to seduce me?"

The corners of his mouth lifted, adding a deep twinkle to his already glowing eyes. "And here I'm thinking it's the other way around."

She stood silent in front of him. Licking her lips while her mind raced with uncertainty. Why didn't he kiss her? Why didn't he finish what he'd started? What was he waiting for?

Right in the middle of her thoughts, he moved toward the pool edge. Then hoisted his body over the side and climbed out. After grabbing a couple of towels from the pool house, he waited for her to get out, then tossed her a towel.

The moment was gone. In awkward silence, she pressed the towel against her wet shorts and blouse.

He threw his towel over his shoulder, turned his back on her, and took the path to the house.

Clare plopped down onto the chair Will had recently vacated. She sat motionless as the sun bathed its warm rays over her damp clothes.

She hated dishonesty. She ran her fingers through her semi-wet hair. *Little lies always turn into big ones.* Little white lies. She shook her head. *White.* How stupid. They always mushroomed into something one never intended. Little or big. Didn't matter. A lie was a lie. Nothing white about them.

She stood, still determined to find another way off the island. That hadn't changed. She left the pool and took the path to the ocean.

After twenty minutes of walking, she was about to give up when she saw a boat dock in the distance. She wanted to dance a jig but instead, broke into a run.

Hampered by the soft sand, it took longer to reach than she first thought. Sweat peppered her flesh. She stumbled, then huffed out a breath, brushing her damp hair from her face in one quick motion.

As she caught her breath, she spied a small boatyard, a shed off to the right and could see several boats tethered at the dock. A dinghy and two sailboats.

"Clare."

She spun at the sound of Will's voice just as she passed the boat yard. Darn it. How in the world? Clamping her lips together, she trudged on.

* * *

"Clare!" Will sprung after her. He didn't think she'd actually try to take the dinghy, but he was still far enough away that he wasn't certain.

She skidded to a halt near the first sailboat, then slowly turned toward him. Her chest heaved while she caught her breath. His long strides closed the distance in seconds.

With hands on hips, the corners of her lovely mouth lifted, revealing a saucy grin. She started to say something, but the words died away along with her smile. She stood transfixed and stared past him at the *Palm Pilot*.

In an instant, he knew something was wrong. His gut told him to make light of the situation. "Solid Burma teak. She's beautiful, isn't she? If you're thinking of taking her out, you can't. I've been working on her for some time now, but there're still a few things in need of repair before she's sea worthy."

"How is this possible?" she choked out, taking a tentative step forward, then another.

"How is *what* possible?"

She spread one hand over her heart. A mixture of sorrow and unbelief etched across her features. She turned to him, her eyes searching his face as if he had the answer.

He glanced from the boat to her. "I don't understand?"

Had she even heard him? As if in a trance, she moved slowly along the dock, then stepped on board.

Though eerily calm, her expressive eyes held something between shock and sorrow.

He followed her on board, and as she moved to the bow, her right hand stroked the weathered teak as if she'd found a long-lost friend.

"You recognize her?"

She nodded, but didn't speak.

"Did you know the family?"

She didn't respond, just continued down the starboard side, then took the steps down to the compact galley. Once below deck, she turned in a slow circle, her luminous eyes soaking in every detail around her.

"What is it, Clare? You look like you've seen a ghost."

She raised her eyes to his. The anguish etched across her pale face rendered him a one-two punch.

"Where did you get it?" Her voice wobbled.

"I bought it years ago. It belonged to James Pendelikon," he said. "But I think you already know that."

"You *bought* it from him?"

"Yes. It was in dry dock for several years, until I finally had time to work on it. I just had it put back in the water a few days ago."

"So it was broken?"

"Clare, I think you're in shock. Let's go back to the house. We can talk there."

"No. No. I'm all right." She scrambled up the steps and tripped halfway up. He snaked out a hand to steady her, but she flung it off.

Completely dumbfounded, Will exited the *Palm Pilot* and followed after her. He stayed with her, but hung back. It was obvious she needed time alone. She must have known the Pendelikons. There was no other explanation for her odd behavior.

He followed her inside and wasn't surprised to see her heading upstairs for the bedroom. He'd just closed the gap between them when she shut the door in his face.

"Clare." He tapped lightly on the door. And then again. But no answer. He tried the door handle, but it was locked.

He stood outside the door pondering his next move. Haunted by her stricken look, he made a decision.

He entered the bedroom next to Clare's and pushed the upper left side of the secret-paneled door. A light click cut through the quiet, then the door released. He pushed lightly so as not to startle her and went in. The door opened to the right of the closet near the corner wall.

Clare was sitting up in the bed, eyes closed with her fingers splayed across her forehead.

He entered the room, then stopped, uncertain whether or not he'd be welcome. He took a chance and sat down on the edge of the bed next to her. It was all he could do not to take her in his arms.

"Clare."

No answer.

"Clare, what's wrong? It's obvious seeing the boat here has upset you."

She lowered her hands and pinned him with an intense stare. "How did you get it? Tell me, now!"

"I told you. I bought it from James Pendelikon."

"You're a lair. He would never have sold it."

He sucked in a breath and stared at her, anger simmering beneath the surface. He clenched his jaw and held himself in check. She was distraught, but it didn't lessen her brash remark.

"And you know that, how?"

She refused to answer, just continued to stare at him with her glistening tear-filled eyes.

"What was your relationship to them?"

No answer.

He stood and shoved his hands in his pockets. "I'd be happy to show you the bill of sale."

She sprung off the bed onto her feet. "I'd like to leave."

Tension surrounded them as they stood facing each other. "Alphonse will be here tomorrow afternoon. You can leave then."

He put his back to her, then strode from the room.

Will clipped down the stairs and headed for the wet bar. Thirty seconds later, he tossed one square ice cube, then an ample amount of golden fire into a glass. Eagle Rare, two fingers deep, waited patiently in the tumbler.

He could hear his father now, instructing him and Wes, *Let it wait. Don't be too quick to knock it down. It's to be enjoyed. Savored.*

The rich, spicy, clove and wood smoke of MacCallan 18 Single-Malt Scotch had been his father's choice. But Will preferred the toasty, honey-wheat seduction of bourbon.

He sat down and lifted the glass to his lips, allowing the creamy, complex mixture to roll across his tongue.

He huffed out an angry breath and leaned back against the sofa, staring at the ceiling as if he'd find answers there.

Clare Sullivan got more and more interesting and aggravating by the second. Her emotional response was not unlike his mother's when she'd heard the news that day ten years ago. Shocked and dismayed, her biggest concern had been for James and Rachel's two daughters.

If seeing the boat hit Clare this hard, then she must have been very close to the family. But why would she care if it had been sold? More than that, what business was it of hers, anyway?

He cradled the tumbler in his hands. James Pendelikon had been a formidable character. Bigger than life. Engaging and personable from the moment he and Wes had met him.

When Pendelikon agreed to be on their board of directors, they'd been elated. They knew if anyone could help save Carrington Coffee, it would be him. And he had. In the few board meetings he'd attended before his death, his advice and expertise corrected their course, setting in motion the things necessary to bring Carrington Coffee from the red into the black.

Maybe at some point Clare could introduce him to the sisters. He'd like nothing better than to meet them and tell them what their father had done for Carrington Coffee.

He pushed himself off the sofa and stood. Alphonse would return tomorrow with the cruiser. He'd apologize to Clare and see if they could begin again. There was still so much he wanted to know about her. *Needed* to know.

CHAPTER TWENTY

Clare stood at the door to Edward's suite and knocked.

"Miss Clare. Twice in one week? I'm honored." He bowed.

"Don't ever change, Edward. No matter how hard I try to bully you into it."

"I wouldn't think of it. May I get you a drink or chocolate candy?"

She sat down and raised her eyes to his twinkling brown ones. "You know me so well. But no thanks."

"Ah, so it's advice you need."

"What makes you say that?"

"There've only been two reasons you ever visited me in my private quarters. Board games and chocolate, or for *advice* and chocolate."

"You mean, chocolate and peanut butter, don't you?"

He nodded. "I have not forgotten."

She tucked her feet beneath her. "When Mom and I moved in after she and Dad got married, I was terrified. The house was so big and way up in the sky."

Edward folded his newspaper and gave her his full attention. "I remember. You were especially frightened of the balcony."

"Yes."

She fiddled with the hem of her blouse. "And then you discovered my penchant for Reese's cups and tea parties."

He smiled, stood up, and strolled to a nearby cabinet.

"Remember when you set up the tea party in the center of the balcony and had at least twenty unwrapped Reese's cups resting on the three-tiered tray?"

His back was to her and when he turned, he was holding two orange-wrapped squares.

"They've been waiting for your return." Edward sat down and handed her one. They unwrapped the peanut butter candy in silence, then lifted the milk chocolate coating to their lips.

"You have no idea how difficult it was not to lick my fingers after unwrapping twenty peanut butter cups in the hot sun," he said.

"Oh, come on." She licked chocolate off one of her fingers. "You know you did."

"On the contrary, I exhibited the utmost in self-control. And then the chocolate started to melt and I began to wonder if you'd ever come out."

"But I did. It's pathetic when I think that's all it took. Seriously. Peanut butter cups?"

"You were six. Nothing pathetic about it. Soon, you were smiling and laughing with no thought of the balcony and the five floors beneath us."

"It was the ocean that scared me. To see it span for miles like that. I'd never seen it from that height."

"What do you think of the view now?"

"Breathtaking. It makes me feel insignificant, yet special all at the same time."

Edward finished his candy and looked at her. "What's on your mind, Clare? As much as I'd like to think you came for chocolate and peanut butter, I feel something's been bothering you lately. Is it that young man you told me about?"

"It's about the *Palm Pilot*."

The light faded in Edward's eyes. Regret took its place as he gazed at her for more information. "What about it?"

"I found it."

"What?"

"The man I've told you about, he has it. Says Dad sold it to him. But I know he'd never have sold it. He knew how much I loved it. I'd always thought he was going to give it to me. I mean, we raced in her. Won the Sunset Harbor Regatta three years in a row with her. Did he ever say anything to you about selling it?"

He shook his head. "I can't recall Mr. Pendelikon ever mentioning it. At least, not in my presence. Which doesn't mean much. I wasn't his confidant."

"You mean like us?"

"Exactly."

She gave his arm a quick squeeze.

"Who bought it?"

"Will Carrington."

"Of Carrington Coffee?"

"Yes."

"Not long before your parents died, your father was on Carrington Coffee's board."

"What?"

Edward nodded. "He and Joseph Carrington were long-time business associates and after Mr. Carrington died, the chairman of their company approached Mr. Pendelikon about joining the board of directors."

"Oh, my gosh. I had no idea we had that connection."

"If I remember correctly, your father attended several board meetings before he and your mother passed away."

"So Dad must have sold the *Pilot* to Will right before he died." She shook her head and sighed. "So much has been lost. And I've made such a mess of things."

"Any chance you're referring to Will Carrington?"

"There's definitely that chance."

"Is he your Jekyll and Hyde?"

She nodded.

"And does this have anything to do with him buying the *Pilot*?"

"It's much more complicated than that."

"Do you love him?"

"He's an arrogant womanizer."

"But do you love him?"

"Yes."

"I see."

"That's where I was over the weekend. The Carrington Estate in the Keys. We had an argument, then today before I left he told me he wanted to start over. But I'm afraid my response was far from cooperative."

"Snarky, were you?"

She rolled her eyes and nodded. "But now, I'm not sure I made the right decision. Oh, I don't know." She stood and began to pace. "There's still so much he doesn't know. And I've gotten in so deep I'm not sure he'll ever forgive me." She stopped mid-stride. "Why do things have to hurt so badly?"

"The good book says it rains on the just *and* the un-just."

"I've never heard you quote scripture before."

"I tend to be private when it comes to my faith, but it doesn't mean I don't have any. I read the Bible every morning and every night."

She plopped back down next to him. "So that's what makes you such a good and fair man."

"I'm happy you think so."

Clare rested her head on his shoulder. "Oh, Edward. I've deceived him. And I don't know how to fix it."

"I'm always here for you, Miss Clare. Now what's this mess that can't be fixed?"

CHAPTER TWENTY-ONE

"Will, I'd like you to meet Megan. Megan, my brother, Will."

Chris had been hounding him to meet his beloved Megan for weeks. "Then you can see for yourself she's not after my money," he'd said. "Besides, it's in trust until I'm twenty-five. That's years from now."

There was truth in that statement, and if he and Wes thought they could keep their younger twin brothers from dating, they were crazy. But caution was still necessary, and it wouldn't be the first time he and Wes had to stop a possible fortune hunter.

A petite blonde, dressed in a yellow sundress, strolled through his office door and extended her hand. He could certainly see why Chris was enthralled with her. Her engaging smile and glowing eyes said it all.

"It's nice to meet you," he said. "Please, have a seat."

"So you're the *nice* big brother."

Will looked to Chris for an explanation.

"Megan didn't want to meet you until I explained there were two of you, and that it was Wes who had the big mouth."

"Of course. You'll have to forgive my twin. He can be overbearing and obnoxious at times."

Megan nodded. "I do understand his wanting to protect Chris from fortune hunters, but there are nicer, less hurtful ways."

"I agree."

"I told you she was special." Chris laid his arm over Megan's shoulder and pulled her to his side.

"You did. *And* she is."

A rosy hue covered Megan's cheeks. If a few compliments could undo Wes's ill-chosen remarks, then he was happy to oblige. Both Cal and Chris deserved normalcy in their lives, and this constant eagle eye of Wes's needed to stop, or at the least, tone down a bit. Will saw nothing wrong with Chris's girlfriend, but he'd agreed to this meeting to make certain there was indeed nothing to worry about.

"So, have a seat and tell me about yourself." He watched with some amusement as she took her seat with all the grace of a princess. The slight tilt of her chin, with her hands clasped neatly in her lap, Megan demonstrated a most proper upbringing. For a fleeting moment, she reminded him of someone else.

"Well, like Chris, I also lost my parents when I was ten."

He nodded. "Chris *did* mention that. I'm sure that was a tough time for you."

"It was." Chris squeezed her hand, and she smiled adoringly at his younger brother. "*And* we were both raised by an older sibling. Well, in my case, a sibling and a butler."

"A butler? Nice."

"He is, actually. He's sort of like a father, I guess. But in a stand-offish, semi-adoring sort of way." She laughed.

There it was again, a familiarity that he couldn't quite place. For a split second he stared at her. Puzzled, his brain searched through his memory bank. He'd almost had it, then the moment was gone.

"So, you have a sister."

"Yes, she's—"

"Bossy, controlling, and a real pill—" Chris said.

"No, she's not. Well, maybe sometimes." Megan giggled. "She had concerns about you, too."

"What?" he scoffed. "She thought I was after your money, right?"

"No, *I* was more concerned about that," Megan said.

Chris's jaw dropped.

A dimple appeared at the side of her mouth. "Oh, not after I got to know you, of course."

Good save, sweetheart.

Megan's smile broadened as she gazed at his younger brother, and Will slouched back in the chair to enjoy the show. They bantered, flirted, and argued like lovebirds on a branch. Like the unseasoned college freshmen they were.

They had a lot to learn about relationships. But they seemed to be off to a good start. Chris certainly appeared older and more mature than the last time he'd seen him. Maybe a girlfriend would be good for him.

"Then what *is* her problem with me?" Chris said.

"I'm sure it's nothing to do with you. She was just angry about Wes's remarks." Megan pursed her pink lips.

"I can't say that I blame her," Will said.

"Now that I think about it..." Megan paused and stared ahead of her. "She was pretty mad."

"Would it help if I talked with her?" Will leaned forward and linked his fingers together. "I'd hate for her to think so badly about us."

"Well," Chris said. "After she caught us making—"

"Chris!" Megan's eyes widened, then darted in his direction.

"Oh, he doesn't care," Chris said.

"Well, *I* care." Megan frowned and fixed Chris with a stare.

Chris shook his head as if he were dealing with a silly child. "Her sister caught us in a *slightly* compromising position."

"Chris!" Megan wailed, then turned wide eyes toward Will. "I promise, nothing happened."

"That's exactly right and that's why he doesn't care," Chris said.

"Chris, you're embarrassing Megan." And just when he thought Chris was showing signs of maturing.

Megan stared at him, pink-cheeked and flustered.

"As I was saying..." Will gave his brother the eye, then turned his attention back to Megan. "Let me know if you'd like me to talk with her." He fervently hoped he'd changed the subject.

"I might take you up on that." Megan sighed. "She seems to think Wes is having Chris watched."

"Wes would never do something like that," Chris interjected with a bravado that fell flat.

"I'm sure Wes is not having Chris followed." Will spoke directly at Megan and smiled. But truthfully, it would be just like his control-freak twin to put Chris and Cal under surveillance. And if that were the case, he'd certainly handle his twin. But whether or not he could convince a suspicious older sister that nothing could be further from the truth was another matter.

Thirty minutes later, Will escorted Chris and Megan to the elevator.

"I'd be happy to talk with your sister, Megan. Or meet with her if she'd prefer. Just let me know."

Megan brightened. "Thanks. Chris and I might need your intervention."

Will waited until the elevator door closed. He liked Megan. She was bright, thoughtful, and yes, adorable. He saw nothing wrong with Chris dating her. Having a steady girl could be good for him. He also noticed Chris had withheld Megan's last name. What was his little brother holding back?

Fine. He could deal with that. *Nothing wrong with having a few secrets.*

He put his back to the elevator and headed to his office. What was it about the Carrington men that seemed to attract secretive women? He had no worries as to her intentions regarding Chris's money. She was obviously well off. How many people in today's time have a butler?

He'd been tempted to ask what line of work her father had been in, but decided not to press her. He felt like he'd given her the third degree as it was. Plenty of time to find out more about her. Besides, they were college freshmen and probably wouldn't be dating that long.

Chapter Twenty-Two

After her heart to heart with Edward, Clare knew she needed to make an attempt to set things right with Will.

Squaring her shoulders, she entered the offices of Carrington Coffee and approached Carol's desk. "Hey, Carol, I know I'm early. Is he in?"

"Hey, Clare." Carol's warm reception put Clare somewhat at ease. "He just got back." Carol got up and poked her head in Will's office. "Clare's here."

Carol turned to her. "Go on in."

Clare sucked in a breath, slowly let it out, then entered Will's office. He was standing by his desk. She stopped and waited for him to speak first. After her final parting words when she'd left the island, she wasn't sure if she'd be welcome.

"Hello, Clare. Please sit down."

"Thanks for seeing me." She took the seat by the window and waited for him to join her.

"I have to say, after your refusal of my offer to *start over*, I'm surprised to see you here."

"I know."

"Wait. Don't tell me. Has hell frozen over?"

"You're not about to make this easy for me, are you?"

"I'm listening."

She swallowed. "There are some things... a *lot* of things, I need to explain. First of all, I'd like to help your grandmother with her little house. Free of charge. After the gold rush thing, it's the least I can do. So, I was wondering if I could come back when she's *actually* there and meet with her?"

"I'm sure she'd like that."

"Does this Saturday work?" She held her breath and waited for his reply.

"Sure."

"Good. Um. I was hoping we could talk while I was there. I have a great deal to say, and it's somewhat complicated for me to spill it all out right now."

She could tell he was having difficulty trusting her motives. Yes, she wanted to get back on board the *Palm Pilot*, but she couldn't very well tell him that. That would lead to questions, but she had questions of her own that needed to be answered first.

"Why such a hurry to come back? As I recall, you couldn't wait to leave the last time you were there."

"Can you blame me? I was pretty much kidnapped."

He gnawed the inside of his lip and eyed her with what seemed to be a growing suspicion. "I could have my grandmother come up here if you'd like?"

"No. No. I'd prefer to see her and the house together. It's how I like to work."

He stepped forward and gently took hold of one of her hands. "Is this your way of saying you want to give us another go? Or are you still playing games?"

She licked her lips and gazed into his sincere eyes. The Will she'd come to love had honest eyes and, more importantly, her heart. But he seemed to be two different people. And now she'd discovered he'd had her father's boat, *her* boat, for years. She was tired of the confusion, the lies. She needed answers. "I'm not playing games."

"I think you know how I feel about you. If you don't, then you've been on another planet."

She couldn't hold back her smile. "I feel the same way, but there're still some things between us. I can't commit to anything until we've talked. I haven't been totally straight with you, and—"

"Shh." He placed his finger over her lips. "I have a meeting in less than ten minutes and right now all I want to do is this."

He folded her in his arms and kissed her. Her confessions could wait until Saturday. She melted against him. This suited her just fine.

* * *

"I see he apologized." Will's grandmother clasped Clare's hand into her frail one. "Good."

Clare glanced at Will. Eyes twinkling, he gazed fondly at the sweet woman, and didn't seem at all perturbed at her reprimand.

"I'm afraid I'm the one who needs to apologize," Clare said.

"No, dear. It's always the man who's wrong." She winked. "Your room's ready. But first we'll have tea on the veranda."

"My room?"

"Yes. You're staying the weekend."

Clare opened her mouth to speak, but Will beat her to it.

"She's only staying until after dinner, Grandmother."

"Nonsense. I have the rest of the weekend planned, plus Sophia has already prepared your room. But first, tea."

She led Clare through the house to one of the side porches where tea was already waiting.

"This is awfully kind of you, Mrs. Carrington, but—"

"Please call me Mary." Mary Carrington settled into a white wicker chair and poured tea into the two cups. "Now, what would you like to know?"

Clare blinked and stared at the forthright little old lady sitting next to her.

"My likes, my dislikes, my lifestyle?" Mary said.

Clare took a hasty sip of her tea, now lukewarm, and set the cup on the table in front of her. "Okay, well, let's see. Do you have a color scheme in mind?"

"I'm quite fond of blue, and I like the color of the sand and the ocean at sunset."

"That sounds lovely," Clare said.

"And a touch of green would be nice or some yellow."

"Both would work very nicely with blue."

Will's phone buzzed from his pocket. "Excuse me, ladies." He left them as they turned their discussion to the pros and cons of using wicker or white-washed pine. Good, hopefully he'd leave them to it.

Two minutes later, he reappeared. "Alphonse needs me in Key West. I may not get back until after dinner. That all right with you two?"

"Of course," Mary said. "This is girl talk anyway." She shooed him away with the flick of her delicate hand.

"Dismissed like a schoolboy." Will's eyes filled with humor. "Thank you, Grandmother."

He was certainly the charmer when he wanted to be. His two-faced act still a riddle she'd like to solve. Will Carrington made her nervous and giddy at the same time, and she didn't need him anywhere near her at the moment. Plus, she hadn't yet figured out how she was going to explain the events and her actions over the past two months. But before she did, she needed to get back on board the *Pilot*.

Good thing he was leaving for the rest of the day. Even though he'd said they were *starting over*, she had the distinct feeling he was monitoring her. She couldn't blame him for not trusting her. After all, she had an ulterior motive to coming back here. There was no way he would know that of course. And it wasn't like it was sinister or anything. She wanted to get back on the *Palm Pilot*, and Mary Carrington wanted her to decorate her cottage. A win-win as far as Clare was concerned.

As she talked color and fabrics with Mary, her mind strayed to the *Palm Pilot*. With so many unanswered questions, she found it difficult to concentrate.

Truthfully, she'd thought of little else but getting back on board since she'd arrived that afternoon. Her need to find answers to that awful day drove her to finish up with Mary as quickly as she could.

After one of Sophia's marvelous dinners, Mary retired for the evening. That worked for Clare. She'd let Mary think she'd retired as well. When she was sure the house was asleep, she'd make her way to the *Pilot*. And hopefully, she wouldn't have to deal with Will until tomorrow.

She waited until well after midnight before she left the house. By now, Will had probably returned and was snug in his own bed.

With a slow turn of the knob, she opened the bedroom door. A creak, like tired worn-out knees, penetrated the dark hallway. She hadn't noticed that earlier in the day and was certain the sound had to have awakened the house.

She clamped her teeth shut and breathed a silent prayer, hoping no one heard. She crept from the bedroom with the stealth of a seasoned burglar, tiptoed downstairs, then went out the back door.

Once outside, she flicked on the flashlight. The walk to the boat seemed longer in the dark. She gazed upward. A million stars winked and sparkled down at her, while the heady scent of jasmine reminded her of Will's kiss by the pool.

She swallowed and continued on.

Approaching the dock, she scanned the starboard side of the *Pilot* with her flashlight. A sudden ache penetrated her heart at the sight of the beautiful, aged teak. A ghostly aura surrounded the *Pilot* with all the magic of a Hollywood fantasy film. Seeing her moored in the dark, with saltwater gently smacking her sides and soft night sounds all around her, Clare savored the moment.

"Hello gorgeous." She greeted the *Palm* in a husky whisper as she stepped on board.

The familiar creak of deck beneath her feet would have normally been a welcoming sound, but at two in the morning it made her heart pound. What was it about the dark of night that made one think the worst?

She scanned the mast with the flashlight. She knew exactly where the crack had been, but it was gone. Will must have repaired or replaced the mast. She yearned to know the facts of that day. When she talked with him tomorrow, she'd find out everything. Then she'd know.

After her father sold Will the boat, he must have wanted to take it out one more time. He'd proposed to her mother on the *Pilot*. Clare still didn't understand why he would have sold it. When it was never returned, she'd assumed it had sunk on the day of the accident. At sixteen, it had been a double loss.

She inched her way below deck and flicked on the cabin light. She'd planned to sneak away during the day to get on board, but after her decision to stay the weekend, she'd decided a late night visit would be less conspicuous. It's not that she cared if anyone knew, it was solely for privacy. She wasn't ready to bare her heart to anyone regarding that day and what this boat meant to her. She simply sought healing.

Closure.

Peace.

She hoped the dull light from the cabin wasn't noticeable from the house. Not that anyone would be awake at this hour.

She'd been stunned to discover the *Palm Pilot* was sound and sea worthy and docked at the Carrington estate. Maddening to know it had been here all these years and she hadn't known it.

Her stepfather had called her a fine sailor. But it hadn't been the first time she'd been irresponsible with the boat. Fine sailor skills or not, her stepfather had threatened to sell it if she didn't take better care of it.

Well, Will Carrington owned it, so her father had obviously gone through with his threat. The day she'd noticed the mast was cracked, she was determined to have it repaired herself, then let her father know it had been taken care of.

But, caught up in school and her teen girl activities, she'd forgotten all about it.

When Will agreed with her plan to help his grandmother, her heart sang with the prospect of getting back on board. Tomorrow afternoon, she'd invite Will for a long walk and tell him everything.

She moved slowly through the cabin taking in every detail of the compact space. She was much calmer now that the initial shock was behind her.

The narrow stack of drawers sat nestled between the two lower bunks like they always had been. She pulled open the top drawer and peered inside. A couple of pens and a tablet were next to a box of tissue. She opened the second drawer, then the third. Between the two, they housed a bit of makeup and a few personal things of her fathers. A flashlight and…

Oh, my gosh!

She sucked in a delighted breath, gazing down at her pearl-handled knife. She smiled, unable to contain her happiness.

Over the years, she'd often wondered what had happened to it. She'd completely forgotten it had been on the boat. She rubbed her thumb over the handle. The pearl luster warmed her fingers, flooding her mind with a slew of memories.

She was on her father's lap when he'd told her he had a special gift for her. When he'd placed it in her hand, he'd dove into a litany of safety rules regarding the small weapon. She'd felt so grown up. So very special. She could still recall the twinkle in his eye when her mother had objected.

She turned the knife over in her hands, then slipped it safely in her shorts pocket. She yanked open the bottom drawer. Empty. Closing it, she straightened and turned around.

"I take it this is the real reason you wanted to come back."

Clare sucked in a sharp breath. "Oh, God. Will. You scared me half to death. Why didn't you let me know you were there?"

"And interrupt your...*perusal*?"

His eyes accused in the low light of the cabin.

"I realize how this must look."

He opened his palm. "Hand it over."

She gazed at him, perplexed at first, then it dawned on her. She reached into her pocket, pulled out the delicate knife, and placed it gently in his hand. "Would you believe me if I told you it was mine?"

"Then why sneak out in the middle of the night?"

"I didn't want to wake anyone, that's all." What a lame excuse.

The light of the cabin accentuated his tightened jaw. "And your desire to help my grandmother. Was that a lie? And the things you said to me at the office the other day. Lies, as well?"

"No."

He barked a harsh laugh. "Well. I guess time will tell." He pursed his lips. "Come on. Let's go."

She hesitated, wondering if she should tell him again the knife was hers. But it was too soon for explanations and much too late for confessions. Maybe he'd be in a better mood for listening tomorrow. She hoped so.

He swept his arm toward the upper deck. "After you."

He didn't say a word as they made their way back to the main house. She glanced once at his profile as they mounted the stairs. His face was stone cold. She could hardly blame him. She did look like a thief.

He paused at her door and waited for her to enter. After she stepped inside, she turned toward him, but he'd already disappeared down the hall.

* * *

The following morning, after a night of tossing and turning, Clare came down to breakfast. She was anxious to talk to Will. She cared deeply for him and wanted to set the record straight about her actions *and* his.

When she entered the kitchen, Mary approached her and took Clare's hands between her frail ones.

Something was wrong.

"I'm so sorry you have to leave, dear. I hope everything will be all right at home. You will come back, won't you? We've barely even started on the cottage. I still want to hear all of your ideas."

So, Will had created an emergency for her, giving her no choice, but to leave. He stood gazing at her with utter indifference. It pained her to see him looking at her with such apathy. After last night, she could only imagine what he must be thinking.

She turned her attention back to Mary and patted her frail hands. "I'll certainly try." Clare wanted to assure her, but knew she'd never be welcomed back.

"The cruiser is waiting," Will said.

Clare nodded. "I'm ready. I'll need to get my things—" At that moment, Clare noticed Sophia standing in the hallway, with her purse and briefcase. She gave Mary's hands one last squeeze. "Goodbye."

Clare followed Will to the dock. His cold shoulder treatment was so unlike him. Oh, God. What had she done? If she'd only confronted him about Megan in the very beginning of their relationship, none of this would have ever happened.

"You'll excuse me for not accompanying you to the mainland." His glance cut through her like her pearl-handled knife.

"Don't you want to know why?"

He pulled his gaze from the ocean, then looked right at her. "Not particularly."

She nodded. "I understand." And she did. He saw her as an untrustworthy, on and off gold digger. As for Will? She knew him as two completely different men. And one in particular rocked her world, shook her to her core with his heart-stopping smile and amazing kisses. *That* man she loved. As for the other?

She stared at him. Searching. Wondering. Cold and aloof, he offered nothing. Just as well this was goodbye. She was sure she couldn't live with two such completely different personalities, anyway.

Her eyes lingered on his chiseled features. This was it. This was goodbye. She stepped on board doing her best to stay composed. She dared not look back. She was close to tears, but couldn't figure out what to say to him.

Too much deceit had transpired for her to just blurt everything out at this juncture. Plus, he'd made it clear he didn't want to know. But at some point, he would. He'd be curious. She'd wait for that moment. She'd make an appointment. Tell him everything. Then politely ask for her knife back. After some time, he might even consider selling her the *Palm Pilot*.

She took a seat in the back. Bathing in the Florida sunshine would allow her to keep her sunglasses on. To hide the tears that now fell.

Alphonse pulled the speedboat away from the dock and opened the throttle. The cruiser cut through the glistening water, putting distance between them just as another boat approached on the starboard side.

* * *

When Will made the decision to make Clare leave, he'd told himself there'd be no going back. Even then, it still took every ounce of self-control to keep his hands off her.

This morning she stood in the kitchen looking lovelier than ever. He'd wanted to scoop her into his arms. Cuddle up with her. Nuzzle her slender neck and shoulders. Kiss her glossy lips. But knew if he touched her, it would be all over for him. He'd give her one more chance.

He scoffed at the departing cruiser. He was one slow learner. A fool to trust his heart to a beautiful, scheming woman. By God, he knew just how Wes felt.

Sick at heart, he strode toward the house. He supposed he should be thankful he'd escaped this one. He shook his head. And she'd almost had him convinced, too. But it was all a lie.

The roar of a boat engine stopped him in his tracks. He thought for a second his cruiser had returned, but it was Chris and Megan. They disembarked and strolled hand in hand toward him.

"Who was that who just left?" Megan brushed a golden strand from her cheek. "It looked just like my sister."

"I doubt that." Will was in no mood to discuss Clare Sullivan. "Come on inside you two. Grandmother is anxious to meet you, Megan."

"I'm telling you. That was my sister."

Will glanced at Chris for an explanation.

"It did look a lot like the dragon lady."

Will gazed at the departing boat, swirling the pearl handled knife between his fingers.

"May I see that?" Megan said.

"Sure." He placed the knife in her hand.

"This looks just like..." Megan turned it over and read the near-faded initials embossed in the handle. C.M.S. "Oh, my gosh. Where did you get this?"

"You recognize this knife?"

"Yes. I have one just like it. My father gave both me and my sister one on our tenth birthdays. But, she lost hers years ago."

His mind calculated the clues like fingers on an adding machine. A rock slammed into his gut. "Who are you, Megan? Who was your father?"

She hesitated, looking at Chris as if she needed encouragement. "Well. I guess it's okay to tell you. I keep it a secret from most people I meet."

"What she means is she wants people to like her for *her*, not her money." Chris grinned.

Megan nodded. "I'm Megan Pendelikon. James Pendelikon was my father."

Will's heart stopped. "James Pendelikon? As in Pendelikon the multinational corporation that designs and manufactures airplanes?"

She gave a sheepish grin. "That's the one."

He felt the blood drain from his face. "And your sister's name?"

"Clare Marie Sullivan." She lifted the knife so he could see the three initials. "She's my half-sister. We have the same mom."

So *that's* who Megan had reminded him of. The subtle nuances he'd noticed in Megan were the same ones he'd seen in Clare. "Megan, have I ever said anything to hurt you or insult you in any way?"

"No, but Wes has."

"Does your sister know?"

"Oh, yeah."

"And I assume you told her all about it."

"Of course. I even pointed him out to her when we saw Wes at Osteria Tulia several months ago. At the time I had no idea there were two of you. Other than that, we haven't talked much about it."

I'll.

Be.

Damned.

He glanced toward the water. His cruiser, now a speck in the distance, cut across the gulf. "Do you mind if I keep the knife for a while?"

"Of course, not." Megan handed it to him.

"Let's go inside. We need to have a serious chat. But first, I need to have Alphonse turn that boat around."

CHAPTER TWENTY-THREE

Ten minutes later, Clare stood on the dock, arms folded, ready for battle. She made it a point to keep her sunglasses on. She'd rather die than have him know she'd been crying.

"Will Carrington, you are nothing but a first-class bully. How dare you make him bring me back. Threatening to fire him if he didn't. Would you actually have done that?"

"Of course not." Will sauntered toward her as if he'd all the time in the world. "Alphonse is not only an employee, but a longtime family friend." He shrugged. "I just knew you were listening and trusted in your sense of fairness to cooperate."

"Why, you manipulative—"

"Me? What about you?"

"Hey, am I going to have to separate you two?" Chris stood in the doorway grinning from ear to ear. Megan stood next to him wreathed in smiles.

Clare's jaw dropped. "Megan?"

"Hey, sis." Megan hurried through the front door and grasped Clare's hands. "I knew that was you. I didn't know you two had finally met." Face beaming, she glanced from Will to Clare. "You should have told me. We could have come out together."

"You know this place? You've—"

"Before we go any further, let's all go into the house and get a tall glass of iced tea. I have a few *million* questions of my own." He held the door, keeping his eyes on Clare, while the others stepped across the threshold.

As they entered, Clare grabbed hold of Megan's arm. "Have you been seeing Chris all this time?" she whispered. "And behind my back?"

"I wouldn't put it quite like that. But, what about you? I've never seen you so fired up." Grinning, Megan leaned closer to Clare in a conspiratorial manner. "Looks like you have a few secrets of your own. And from what I've just heard, I'd say you two know each other—

Pretty.

Darn.

Well."

Megan cocked her blonde head to one side. "I'm wondering how that can be since I only told Will about you a few days ago." She raised an expressive brow and waited for an answer.

At that moment, Clare caught the sardonic gleam twinkling in Will's eyes. She pursed her lips and glared at him.

"Megan, I see your older sister keeps secrets from you as well." Will raised a mocking brow as he led the group into the front hallway.

Clare spun toward Megan and wanted to sock her for giggling. "I demand an explanation." She pushed her glasses onto the top of her head. "Start talking—" Clare's eyes widened. "Wait..." She spun toward Will. "You know she's my sister? You didn't tell her about the boat did you? Without me here?"

"What boat?" Megan said.

Clare realized too late she'd made a huge mistake.

"That's one of the million things we need to discuss, but first things first—"

"Clare." Megan touched her sister's shoulder. "Have you been crying?"

Clare sucked in a breath and quickly slid her shades over her eyes. Will stood eyeing her as if trying to come to some conclusion. In one swift motion, he wrapped his fingers around her arm. "Give us a moment." Then he pulled her down the hall to his study. Once inside, he locked the door. "I'm afraid it's you who needs to start talking."

"But the sailboat. What if she—"

"She won't." He shook his head. "Megan was right. You are one pesky mother hen."

Clare's mouth dropped two inches. "Me? Why, when I think about your interference into those kid's lives—"

Right in the middle of her tirade, Will gently slid her sunglasses from her face.

"You *have* been crying."

She yanked her glasses from his hand. "Don't think for a second it's because of you," she spat out.

"All right, I won't." Will leaned against the door, crossed his arms, and waited.

"Unlock that door right now."

Clearly amused, he shook his head, jiggled the key in the air, then slipped it into his pocket. "Not until we have a little chat." He sat down on one side of the sofa, patting the seat next to him. "Come. Confession is good for the soul. And Miss Sullivan, I do believe you have a few things to clear up."

"I have nothing to say to you. And wipe that smile off your face."

"That's not what I heard."

Clare sucked air through her clamped teeth. "What did Megan tell you?"

"Plenty, sweetheart."

She deflated right in front of him.

* * *

"Fine." Refusing to sit, Clare began to pace. Her windblown hair curved appealingly around her face as she crossed back and forth in front of him.

Eyes flashing, her beautiful face clouded over. Her short, but determined strides mesmerized him with every step she took. He loved each turn of her heel, the subtle lift to her chin, and her parted, kissable lips. He loved her. Even in anger, she was everything he'd ever wanted.

"It's just so *hard* to know where to begin." Her voice dripped with sarcasm.

He sat back, and folded his hands in his lap. "Please. Enlighten me."

She drew in a deep breath, then released it. "From day one, you've been against Megan dating Chris. The things you said about her were presumptive and untrue." She continued to pace, slanting a fiery gaze in his direction. "As to your comments at Lenny's, well, 'beyond the pale' doesn't even come close to describing your condescending attitude toward my sister."

From what Megan had recently told him, he knew Clare had confused him with Wes. Will dropped his gaze and focused on an object across the room. There could be no other explanation. He of all people knew how insulting Wes could be. Wes told it like it was and didn't seem to care who he hurt. Will recalled Clare's stormy, accusing eyes at Tulia's and could only imagine how the mix up continued from there. He shook his head. She had no idea he was a twin and that was his own fault.

He refocused his attention on Clare. What kind of woman goes to these extraordinary lengths to deal with a man she believes acted the A-1 jerk to her kid sister?

The kind you love.

Outrageous, unpredictable, spunky. A champion. The kind of woman who'd also fight that same way for him. Gloves off. No holds barred.

Nothing pyrite about this woman. She was gold, all right. Pure, twenty-four Karat.

As he watched her pace, he knew he should put her out of her misery. But she was so darn cute, huffing and puffing. Throwing her arms in the air to make her point.

Adorable in fact. Funny how everything changed when one discovered the truth. For the past twenty-four hours he'd wanted to throttle her. Now he wanted to hold her, to cuddle and kiss her to distraction.

"Thirdly," she continued. "Your arrogance knows no bounds. Your over-the-top comments regarding Megan and women in general were—*are,* disgusting." She stopped right in front of him, chest heaving, eyes sparkling. "Anything else you'd like to know?"

He locked eyes with hers. He needed to know exactly what Wes had said. This wouldn't be the first time he'd have to smooth things over where Wes was concerned. "Could you, ah, remind me again what I said?"

"Like you could forget." She jabbed her fists against her slim hips. "You called her a *gold digger.* More than once, I might add. Told Chris not to bring the *likes of her* to your home *or* your plantation. Why, Megan could buy ten plantations with her inheritance—"

"I know."

"That's... What?" Clare's features creased in confusion.

"You heard correctly.

I.

Know."

She immediately sat. Jaw dropped, she perched on the edge of the chair for three full seconds staring at him, her eyes pouring silent questions from across the room. Then just as suddenly, she regained her poise.

"Of course you know. She's a Pendelikon."

"If it makes you feel any better, I only recently found out, myself."

"Well." She licked her lips. "That doesn't negate the fact that what you said was cruel and hurtful and—"

"Rude and totally uncalled for."

"Right." She clasped her hands together and gave him a somewhat blank stare. "Well, aren't we suddenly amiable?"

He sat there, gazing at her, drinking her in.

"And quit looking at me like you've discovered gold or something." Uncertainty clouded her pretty face. "What are you staring at?"

"You. I *suddenly* like looking at you." He smiled slightly.

She blinked, then lowered her eyes to her lap. "Stop trying to confuse me. It's obvious you now have some sort of relationship with Megan. I'm assuming you've already apologized and set things to right."

He shook his head. "I have not."

Clare's head jerked up. Just as she opened her mouth to speak, the door opened behind her. Megan stood on the threshold. Clare glanced back at Will, an accusatory gleam in her eyes.

"Sorry to deceive you," he said. "That lock's been broken for years. It was the only thing I could think of to get you to stay."

Clare huffed out an impatient sigh as she waited for Megan to speak.

"Clare. Will didn't apologize because it wasn't Will who said those things."

"What do you mean it wasn't Will? Two months ago, with all the drama of a scorned heroine, you pointed *this* man out to me as the greatest villain on the planet." Her chest heaved as she sucked in air. "Now you're telling me it wasn't him?"

"I know. I thought it was Will, too. But later, I found out it was Wes—"

"Wes? Who the heck is Wes?"

"My evil twin," Will said.

"That's right," Megan added. "It was Wes who said those awful things. Not Will."

Clare turned toward Will, eyes accusing, and shot to her feet. "You're a twin? I thought Chris was the twin."

"He is, but so am I."

She spun to face Megan. "And when were you going to tell me this?"

"I don't know." Megan shrugged. "I didn't realize you two even knew each other."

Clare pressed her fingers into her forehead and briefly closed her eyes.

"How was I to know you two were going to meet, much less hook up?" Megan said.

"We have *not* hooked up." Clare spun toward Will. "Tell her."

"I don't know. Does kissing count?"

Megan's eyes lit up like a Christmas tree. "Finally." Megan rolled her eyes. "She hasn't kissed anyone in years."

"Megan!" Clare's voice squeaked an octave higher.

"It's true. When was the last time you had a date?"

Clare opened her mouth, then clamped it shut.

"If you have to think about it, then it's been way too long."

"There is some truth to that," Will said.

Clare briefly squeezed her eyes shut. "I'm his decorator."

"*Was*," Will said. "I fired you, remember?"

"Fired?" Megan's face clouded in confusion. "Why? Clare's the best."

"Let's just say I didn't have the same affinity for gold that she did."

Megan's eyes widened. "That gold digger theme party. The "plotting revenge" party. That was for him? You...you actually went through with it?" Megan burst out laughing.

Clare nodded, flushing a rosy pink.

"Oh, my gosh. I've got to tell Chris."

"I'm glad you think this is funny. If you'd just told me the facts—"

"How was I to know you were embroiled in some insane payback plan?"

Clare slowly crossed her arms. "Like you weren't?"

"Oh, that. I've already explained myself to Chris. And now that he knows who I am, he thinks my actions were adorable."

Clare threw up her hands. "Just stop." She jabbed a finger at Will. "Was he or was he not the man I overheard at Lenny's Sandwich Shop?"

Megan shook her head. "I'm so sorry. I can see I made a mess of things by not telling you. But, I had no idea you were out for revenge. That is so not like you."

"Oh, I beg to disagree," Will said.

* * *

Clare glared at Will, but her forced bravado couldn't outlast the mocking twinkle in his eyes.

"Please, continue." Will settled back in his chair. "I haven't been this entertained in months."

Completely undone, she let out an exasperated breath. In that moment, her insides shrank and she stared at the floor. She felt like an idiot. She'd not only acted like one of those high school mean girls you see on TV, but apparently had done it all against an innocent man.

Will was enjoying himself at her expense, and she knew it was no more than she deserved. Misunderstanding or not, it was she who needed to apologize. What a fool she'd been.

"Will's right, Megan. I'm afraid this entire farce is more like me than you realize. All I can say is I had a totally, and completely, insane moment. I *was* planning on revenge, and I didn't want you to be a part of that. And then..." Clare twisted her hands together. "I *wasn't* going to." She stole another glance at Will and almost died on the spot at the love in his eyes. And wondered for a second if she was seeing things.

Her knees suddenly turned to jelly, and she plopped down onto the loveseat. "I was like a blasted yo-yo. One minute I was out for blood and the next..." She threw up her hands. "It's so complicated."

"Megan, I think I've got this from here," Will said.

Megan grinned and pulled the door closed behind her.

After Megan left, Will pushed himself from the chair, crossed the room, then stopped in front of Clare. She sat, hands clasped, staring up at him.

"Now. If I may have a moment to clear up a few things?"

Clare licked her lips and nodded.

"Good." He sat down next to her. "First of all, I've never in my life eaten at Lenny's Sandwich Shop, so it had to have been Wes you overheard. And from the sound of it, it must have been quite painful for you."

She nodded. "That explains why you didn't recognize me that day."

"Shouldn't that have been a clue that it wasn't me?"

"If I'd known there were two of you, then yes. But since I didn't..." She pinned him with a disgruntled stare.

"You're absolutely right. The fault was *all* mine." His eyes twinkled in merriment.

"Oh, please."

He chuckled. "So, how close were you sitting to them?"

"They were in the booth right next to mine. I was hidden behind the lattice separating the seats."

"So you were eavesdropping?"

"I... Yes, I was. But, not intentionally. I was going to let you—*him*—know I was there, but as soon as he opened his despicable mouth..." Tears pooled in her eyes and she gazed at him. "All I could think of was, how could he? How could the man I'd fallen in love with be this arrogant, chauvinist jerk?"

"You love me?"

"Yes, dammit."

He tenderly took hold of her hands. "Sweetheart, Wes and I are not the same person. I'm not trying to make excuses for him, but he was hurt badly in a relationship." He gave her hands a quick squeeze.

"Why didn't you just tell me you were a twin?"

"I know. I now realize I should have. But, in my defense, the fact that Wes and I *are* twins has been used against us by more than one beautiful, fortune-seeking female. Once, a particular woman who'd gotten nowhere with Wes, turned her sights on me. Neither one of us realized it at the time. My shrewd brother hadn't been deceived, but I, on the other hand, had been taken for a merry ride."

As he spoke, he gathered her in his arms. "I'm happy to regale you with more details later on, but right now, there's only one thing on my mind." He angled his head and gave her a brief, but possessive kiss. "I'm sorry you thought Wes was me." He placed his finger under her chin. "When you said you thought you knew me. Well, you do. The person you thought I was, when I was with you, is who I am."

A suspicious gleam filled her eyes.

He glanced heavenward. "Now what?"

"The first day I came to your office to discuss your project. You were talking on the phone. You called Megan a gold digger. I *know* that was you. So, explain that."

His lips quirked at the corners. "Eavesdropping again?"

"Pretty hard not to, with you in the same room."

He sighed. "That was sarcasm. And if you'd been listening with something other than your pride and anger, you might have picked up on that. Why didn't you say something then?"

"I'd planned to. I was waiting for the right moment to bring it up, but your words made my blood boil."

"I was talking to Wes."

She rolled her eyes. "Him again." She shook her head. "Mr. Carrington. Is it your nature to always blame others?"

"Don't tell me you're getting a soft spot for my despicable, villain of a brother?"

She lifted her shoulder, doing her best to hold back a smile. "Maybe."

Will fixed her with the most delectable, heart-stopping gaze she'd ever experienced and took hold of her hands. "Sweetheart—"

Chris and Megan popped in at that moment.

Will squeezed his eyes shut and huffed out an exasperated breath. "What now?"

"Clare, that was definitely Wes at Lenny's." Chris strolled in. "Trust me, Will would never say such things. The only thing Wes and Will have in common is their looks."

Will shook his head. "Are you two listening through the keyhole?"

"Of course," Megan said.

"No." Chris shot Megan an exasperated glance. "We came to tell you Wes is here."

Clare sighed. And just as they were getting to the good part.

"We'll finish this conversation later." Will squeezed her fingers, and they both stood.

Chapter Twenty-Four

Seconds later, a hushed silence fell over the group as Will's twin sauntered into the library. Wes's smile faltered, and he glanced behind him, as if they'd confused him with someone else.

A roguish twinkle filled his eyes, and his mouth lifted at one corner. "Was it something I said?"

Will chuckled. "On more levels than you realize."

Clare's jaw dropped, and she glanced from him to Wes.

"Uncanny isn't it?" Will said. "Clare. Megan. I'd like you to meet my twin brother, Wes Carrington."

Two sets of feminine eyes glowered at the man who'd just entered the library. Will took a moment to enjoy Wes's discomfort before finally speaking. What brother wouldn't?

Wes smiled a bit uncertainly. Will could tell he was still unsure of his welcome, even if it was in his own home. For a second, Wes extended his hand, but when neither woman reciprocated, he raised it to his chin, quirking a sideways grin. "I'm getting the distinct impression that neither of you ladies like me? Am I in some sort of trouble?"

Clare sucked in a deep breath. *Double* trouble. "You know what they say about first impressions." Clare gritted her teeth. "But you don't seem too perturbed by that fact."

"Well." Wes grinned and leaned forward at the waist. "Let's just say it's not the first time I've been on the receiving end of such a reception."

"Wes, this is Clare Sullivan and her younger sister, Megan Pendelikon." Will finished the introduction, then waited for the light to dawn.

Wes raised an eyebrow and smiled, focusing his attention on Megan. "So *you're* Megan. I see you've managed to wile your way into my kid brother's heart after all."

His smile swiftly faded. "Wait a minute. Did you say, *Pendelikon*? As in airplanes, rockets, and satellites?"

Will burst out laughing. "That took you a bit longer than normal. I'd say you're slipping, brother."

"Well I'll be a son of a..."

"I'd so like to finish that statement," Clare said. "But I've never been one to disparage one's lineage."

"I'm sorry." Wes stared at Clare. "Who are you again?"

Clare raised her adorable chin. "Clare Sullivan. Megan's half-sister."

"Ohhhh, right. So you're the sister *and* Will's latest."

"I'm no one's latest."

Wes glanced at Will and grinned. "I like her."

"So do I," Will said.

Clare blinked and gazed at Will. Her pretty mouth parted as if she was going to say something else, but instead she clamped her lips together.

Wes held out his hand to Megan. "I think I owe you an apology. What do you say? Forgive an over-protective older brother who thinks every pretty girl is out for his younger brother's inheritance?"

Megan dimpled and held out her hand. "I have an over-protective older sister. So I get it."

Will shook his head. Unbelievable. Whether he cut you to the quick or groveled for forgiveness, Wes was a master with words. When he wanted to, he could be damned charming.

Will glanced at Clare who wasn't as easily taken in by Wes's charms. Giving Wes the eagle eye, Clare made a deliberate action of folding her arms, signaling to Wes she would not be so easily swayed.

"Don't think for a second that apology makes everything peachy," she said. "You and I are far from through."

Wes raised an eyebrow. "I can see you're going to be a handful. I think I'll leave *you* to my capable twin."

Clare's jaw dropped. She took one step forward, then stopped, her hands clenched into fists.

Wes winked at Will, then turned his attention to Chris and Megan. "Come on, you two. I have a feeling my safety may be at risk if I stay one second longer." He threw his arms over Chris's and Megan's shoulders and led them into the hallway.

"Hard to believe we're related, isn't it?" Will said.

"I've never hit anyone in my life." Clare stared at Wes's departing back. "But I sure came close to socking him one."

Will laughed. "I feel your pain. Even *I* have to rein him in at times. He's not so bad though, once you get to know him."

"Like that'll ever happen."

"He does mean well. Especially when it comes to Chris and Cal. It's hard to imagine, but when Wes and I were twenty, Wes coached Chris and Cal's little league team. Like a regular family man."

"That *is* hard to believe. So when do I meet Cal?"

"He's flying in next weekend. He's a lot like Wes, so be warned."

"Oh, joy."

Will placed a gentle hand on Clare's back and led her to the sofa. "Enough of my brothers." He pulled her onto his lap. Tipping her chin, he gave her no choice but to look at him. "Now. Where were we?"

"You have a dizzying effect on me, Will Carrington. I feel I have so much to explain, and so much to apologize for, but all I can think about is that you called me *sweetheart.*" She gazed up at him, anticipation and love brimming from her lovely eyes.

"Right." He wrapped his arms around her. "I remember, now."

His mouth covered hers.

Intentional.

Confident.

Staking his rightful claim over her lips and her heart. Clare melted against him. Freely submitting to his declaration without reluctance or timidity.

Moments later, he lifted his head. He devoured her beautiful face, her flushed cheeks, and trembling lips. Then he ran his finger tenderly over her mouth. "I'm so sorry you were confused."

"If you only knew." She shook her head. "My brain is still tied up in knots."

"It never dawned on me you'd mistaken me with Wes."

"Is it any wonder I was a yo-yo where you were concerned?"

"*And* out for blood, don't forget."

Her beautiful eyes glowed, her face radiant. "Oh, that."

"Yes, that."

"When I thought about the things you'd said, or thought you'd said, I'd be so angry and hurt. And then I'd be with you and you'd be so wonderful. Irritating at times, but wonderful."

"Am I wonderful?"

"You know you are."

"God, I love hearing you say that." He kissed the tip of her nose.

"I can't tell you what it's like to truly believe you said all those things, when being with you irrevocably denied them."

"I know, actually."

She chuckled. "Come on. You really thought I was a gold digger?"

"The thought crossed my mind."

"A small price to pay for nearly driving me batty with your Doctor Jekyll and Mister Hyde routine. I'd go from loathing you to simply wanting to win your heart."

"By convincing me you were after my money when all the while you were a Pendelikon heiress?"

Clare flushed a rosy pink he found delightful. She played with a button on her shirt. "I know. I have no excuse for my behavior."

"It's understandable. You thought I was a womanizer. You thought I'd hurt your sister."

"Thanks, but you seem to bring out the high school *mean girl* in me and I must apologize." She ran her finger along his chin. With her doe eyes raised to his, she couldn't hide the twinkle in their depths. She knew exactly what she was doing to him.

His lips curved into a smile. "Apology accepted. But something tells me you missed the normal high school experience." He brushed a wayward strand of hair from her forehead. "Am I right?"

Her faced sobered. "Yes."

He found the whisper in her voice endearing and loved her all the more for her sacrifice.

"I'm certain, like me, you have no regrets."

"None." She sighed. "My best friends didn't get it at all. And before I knew it, I didn't have any close friends. While they partied, I went to parent-teacher conferences and grammar school plays. Speaking of Megan, I need to talk to her, and we're both going to need some answers about the *Palm Pilot*. If she and Chris explore the island and she sees it—"

"I know." He nodded. "Let's go find her."

Chapter Twenty-Five

Clare and Megan stood with arms looped around each other's waist. Clare kept glancing at Megan who hadn't taken her eyes off the sloop since they'd arrived.

"All these years and we never knew." Megan's voice was low and husky.

"I just wish I could have prepared you," Clare said.

Will's heart ached for Clare as she explained having known about the boat for several weeks.

"I was in such a tizzy about everything. I'd planned to tell you I'd found her after I knew more. Forgive me for not letting you know sooner."

"Clare, Clare. Always trying to protect me." She shook her blonde head. "Stop being my mother." Megan gave her a playful shake. "You have nothing to apologize for."

Feeling the need to give Clare support, Will stepped closer and stood beside them. "Your father was our newest board member. We'd had a fantastic board meeting that weekend. Saturday afternoon was free for the board members to enjoy the island and the water. The wind was perfect for sailing. About an hour after your parents went out, the weather took a turn for the worse. The boat they were in capsized. Their bodies were discovered the next day."

"Well, at least you found the sloop."

"We didn't. It was never found."

Clare tore her gaze from the boat. "What do you mean? It's moored right here."

"They didn't take the *Pilot*, they took *my* boat."

"What?"

"Your father noticed a surface crack in the mast of the *Pilot*. I told him I could fix it, so they took my boat."

"Oh, my gosh. Clare." Megan turned to her, grabbed her shoulder, and gave it a good shake. "You know what this means? It wasn't your fault. It was *never* your fault."

Clare stood stunned. "The mast. What was wrong with it?"

"Only a surface crack. It was an easy fix, really."

"You see. You can forgive yourself now," Megan said. "And stop all this nonsense about not taking your inheritance."

Chris laid his hand on Megan's arm. "You okay?"

She smiled sweetly at him and nodded.

"I don't know if you two ladies know this..." Wes's eyes glowed with passion and integrity. "But James Pendelikon saved Carrington Coffee." Wes eyed his twin. "You should tell Clare about it sometime."

Wes turned to Clare. "He was proud of you, you know. Your sailing, your love for the race, whether you won or not."

"What do you mean?"

"You and your father beat us three years in a row at Sunset Harbor's Regatta," Wes said.

Will's jaw dropped. "Of course." He glanced from Wes to Clare. "You were the racing daughter. I'd completely forgotten."

Her eyes lit up. "And that coffee company we always beat, was you?"

Will nodded.

"But, none of this explains why he sold the *Pilot* to you."

"It's like Wes said. Your father was very proud of you. So much so, that he'd planned to buy you an Alden Yacht. When he discovered my love for the older sloops, he sold the *Pilot* to me. I asked him if he thought you'd mind. He told me once he explained about the kind of work I did with vintage boats, you'd be pleased."

Wes got in Will's face. "Do you realize what it would mean if she were on our team next year?" He slapped Will on the shoulder. "Make up with her."

Just as quickly as his serious tone had come, it vanished as he turned to Chris and Megan. "Come on, kids. Let's leave these two alone."

As the three made their way back to the house, Will turned to Clare.

"You all right?"

She raised glistening eyes to his. "Yeah."

He brushed the back of his fingers across her cheek. "And us? Are *we* all right?"

She looked him fully in his face. "I don't know. It depends."

She can't be serious. "On what?"

"On the size of the ring of course." She wrapped her arms around his neck. "If you want me, it'll cost ya."

He gazed down at her laughing eyes and chewed on his lower lip. With one teasing look, she held him spellbound. "Is that so?"

She nodded.

"Okay. How much?"

"Gold. Lots and lots of gold." Her eyes widened. "And one very *huge* diamond." She wiggled the fingers of her left hand in his face.

He tipped his head and eyed her thoughtfully. "You know. This reminds me of something I've been wanting to talk to you about."

"Oh, yeah?" The corners of her mouth lifted.

"I've been thinking about your penchant for mischievous pranks."

"You have?"

"And I hope they never stop."

"Be careful what you wish for, Mr. Carrington."

He cinched her tightly against his chest. "I must admit, I feel quite honored you got to experience your wayward, high school prank days with me."

"I don't know." She cocked her head appealingly to one side. "I think there's just something about you that brings out the worst in me." A dimple appeared next to her mouth.

"Then our life together will be all the more exhilarating."

"Never a dull moment."

"Not for us."

She rose up on her toes and kissed his lips. "I like the sound of that."

"Since you brought up the *R* word, I take it you want to marry me."

"Oh, yes, Mr. Carrington. Don't even think about getting rid of me."

He pulled her close. "Now that that's settled. Tell me more about how you wanted to win my heart."

"How about I show you." Love flowed from her sparkling eyes as her lips covered his.

EPILOGUE

"Oh, Will." Clare stood with her hands over her heart, gazing at her sailboat with wide-eyed appreciation. "She's beautiful."

Will held his breath as he waited for the moment when she'd notice *it*.

She took a few steps to the right, stopped, and sucked in a breath. "You changed her name?"

Gold Rush splayed in bold italic across the stern.

"You don't mind, do you? I thought—"

Clare threw her arms around his neck. "I love it."

Will held her and laughed into her hair. "I'm so glad. I must confess. I had a few anxious moments about the name change. I know how much you loved the *Palm Pilot*."

"No. It's perfect. And we'll sail her together in the next Regatta." She shook her finger in the air. "And beat that brother of yours."

"You bet we will." He banded his arms around her waist, breathing an inward sigh of relief. "Ready to go aboard your wedding gift?"

"Aye, aye, Captain." Glowing with happiness, Clare lifted her hand to her brow and offered a perky salute.

God, she was beautiful and adorable and she belonged to him. "After you, Mrs. Carrington."

"Mrs. Carrington." Batting her gorgeous eyes, she sighed dramatically. "I so love the way that sounds."

He kissed her on the tip of her nose, then released her. "Hopefully you'll still feel that way after you see the changes I made inside."

"Let's go." She took his hand and practically dragged him on board. As they entered the cabin, her eyes lit up in delight. "Oh, my gosh. I can't believe you did all this yourself."

He'd taken out the bunkbeds and the center stack of drawers. A queen bed and slender, floor-to-ceiling, glossy teak cabinets now flanked each side.

"The bed is perfect. And the contemporary built-ins are beautiful. You even modernized the tiny kitchen."

She stepped into his arms. "I love it. Thank you, sweetheart."

Back on deck, they slipped the ropes from the bollards and set sail at sunset. While he was at the helm, Clare came up behind him and slipped her arms around his torso.

"When are you going to tell me where we're going? Leaving this late means it can't be far."

"You're right, it's only a few miles from here."

She ducked underneath his arms and came up in front of him. Standing face to face with him, she settled her hands on his waist. His breath caught at the love in her eyes.

"There's only water a few miles from here," she said.

"You'll see."

She rested her head against his chest. He reveled in her nearness. Her warmth. Her love. He raised one hand to her dark head and laced his fingers through her hair. He was the luckiest man alive. "Don't fall asleep. We're almost there."

She moved out from under his arms. "I'm too excited to sleep," she said, as she gazed out over the water. A warm glow of lights appeared in the distance. "There's an island."

"There sure is."

"Is it yours?"

"No. It's *ours*."

Her mouth dropped open. "You're kidding. Another wedding gift? But, I only gave you my father's gold watch."

"Which I love." He shrugged, smiling. "I just thought we might like a place of our own."

The lights grew brighter as the boat drew nearer to shore. Lanterns hung from lampposts along the dock. They disembarked, and Will took her hand in his.

"Did you do all this?"

"Let's just say I'm responsible for it." He smiled. "Come on."

White twinkle lights circled the trunks of the palm trees along the trail. As they got closer, an array of tropical and flowering plants spread like fingers widening the path to the house. Jasmine and honeysuckle permeated the night air with their sweet scent.

Clare paused, closed her eyes, and took a deep breath. "Do you know what this reminds me of?"

"What, sweetheart?"

"Our kiss by the pool. The weekend you kidnapped me."

He gently squeezed her hand. "I promise. After tonight, you'll have much more than a pool-side kiss to treasure."

Her lashes fluttered over her cheeks. Even though the light was dim, he was certain she was blushing. *My sweet Clare. I promise tonight will be perfect for you.*

He tipped her chin, forcing her to look at him. "You're not nervous are you?"

She pursed her pretty lips. "I'm twenty-six. Just because I haven't *dated*...I've been to *R-rated* movies."

He chuckled. "Then I'm sure you can teach me a few things."

With her head still tilted up at him, her blush was more than evident. He lightly kissed her lips, then took hold of her hand. "Come on."

They meandered along the narrow path until they reached a small white cottage. A comfortable wicker seating area with floral cushions welcomed them as they mounted the porch steps. But it was the inside he couldn't wait for her to see. He'd specifically overseen this part of the surprise himself, wanting every detail to be perfect.

Colorful lanterns and strands of twinkle lights hung across the ceiling of the one-room cottage. Chilled Champagne, dark chocolate, and fresh strawberries waited for them in the small dining area tucked in along the far wall. Clusters of glowing candles sat on rustic tables.

Clare's eyes lit up with laughter.

A sizeable mining tent, the one she'd used in the living room at the gold rush party, stood erected in the middle of the room. The cottage was completely decked out with all the gold rush theme party paraphernalia.

Pressing her palms together, Clare turned her shiny-eyed face toward him. "I wondered what you'd done with all of it. I was sure you'd had it hauled to the dump to be burned."

"After the theme party, I found myself completely unable to part with any of this junk."

"Really?"

"Really." He laughed and scooped her up in his arms. "Okay, wife. You ready to be carried over the threshold?"

"Yes, husband." She laughed with delight as he ducked to enter the tent.

With utmost reverence, he laid her down on the satin-sheeted bed, then stretched out beside her. He propped the side of his head in his hand, gazing at her, his heart bursting with adoration.

Until Clare, he'd had no idea a heart could truly ache for another. Her dark hair splayed enticingly across the satin pillowcase. A sweet case of shyness seemed to overcome her. She glanced down, swallowed and bit her bottom lip. He gently tapped her chin, causing her to look up at him. Her eyes glowed with love and affection. All for him.

Tonight would be all about his Clare. He'd been her first real kiss, and he wanted the rest of her 'firsts' to be just as memorable. Her lack of experience held a special place in his heart. He would not abuse that honor.

He brushed her hair from her forehead. "After the gold rush party, I had a long talk with my grandmother about you."

"You did?"

He toyed with the center button near her heart until it slipped open. "Uh, huh."

"What did she say?"

"That I should make up with you." His fingers slid three inches down to the next button, the one over her heart. It tattooed against his flesh, and his own heart quickened. In that moment he glanced at her face, touched at the trust pouring from her eyes.

Her lips parted in a soft smile. "Wise woman, your grandmother." Her words tumbled out with a breathless sigh.

"She told me you liked me."

"A *very* wise woman." As she spoke, she placed her hand over his fingers. "You're taking *way* too long with this."

He lifted her hand to his mouth and teasingly kissed her fingers. "But, I'm enjoying myself immensely."

She chuckled nervously and brushed a finger along his firm lips. "So am I."

The lanterns spread their warm light, casting a golden glow within the tent. Will gazed at his beautiful bride, drinking in her loveliness. Her eyes sparkled like gems as she shyly fixed her gaze on his in anticipation of what was to come. He gave her a roughish smile, then lowered his mouth to hers.

THANK YOU FOR READING!

Dear Reader,

Thank you for reading, *Double Trouble*. I hope you enjoyed Clare and Will's story as much as I enjoyed writing it.

I need to ask a favor. As you probably know, reviews can be hard to come by. And as a reader your feedback is so important. If you're so inclined, I'd love an honest review of *Double Trouble*. It doesn't have to be long or fancy. :) One or two sentences is fine.

If you have time, here's a link to my author page on Amazon. You can check out all my books here: amazon.com /-/e/B0077AG3ZM

In gratitude,
Darcy Flynn